John P. Becker, Simeon D. Bloodgood

The Sexagenary

Reminiscences of the American revolution

John P. Becker, Simeon D. Bloodgood

The Sexagenary
Reminiscences of the American revolution

ISBN/EAN: 9783337227104

Printed in Europe, USA, Canada, Australia, Japan

Cover: Foto ©Andreas Hilbeck / pixelio.de

More available books at **www.hansebooks.com**

Ph. Schuyler

THE

SEXAGENARY:

or,

Reminiscences of the American Revolution.

Old age prates willingly, as well you know,
And loves to talk about the strange old times
That are no more. ....WIELAND.

ALBANY, N. Y.:

J. MUNSELL, 78 STATE STREET.

1866.

LETTER TO THE PUBLISHER.

J. MUNSELL, ESQ.:

Many years ago, when I resided in the city of Albany, I was frequently attracted to your office, where I found you, combining with the practical industry of printer and publisher, an antiquarian spirit, intent upon the rescue of the traditional and documentary history of that old town. It excited my respect and attention, which have followed you through all your subsequent literary labors. I, too, had been an explorer in the same direction, and you had all the encouragement I could give, to induce you to continue in your career. Since then you have preserved from neglect, if not from oblivion, its very interesting annals, and many local incidents illustrating its progress from its commencement as an outpost of the New Netherland down to its becoming the populous and enterprising capital of a state now containing more inhabitants than the father land. I do not know whether your labors have been appreciated by the people of Albany as fully as they deserve to be, though it is certain they owe to you the rescue of their most interesting monuments, well preserved and cared for, with the inscriptions restored and legible. No one can ever write its history without the careful study, and large use of the *Annals*. More than this, with much originality of design and execution, you have collected a series of curious, valuable, elegantly printed works, illustrating the history of the revolution, snatching from under the crushing footsteps of time, many precious relics which otherwise would have been scattered and lost. As the editor of this remarkable series of works you have gained an enviable reputation.

In complying with your request to furnish you with a copy of *The Sexagenary* to become a part of that series, I do so under the impression that it contains some interesting personal statements, throwing light on the condition of our northern borders during the revolutionary struggle; and it, so far at least, may be a guide to the future writer who shall seek to portray the social aspect of that time. Unfortunately there are but few personal narratives of the period extant, for those were not the days for writing or publishing.

This little work was undertaken at the suggestion of Governor DeWitt Clinton, who, at the same time, placed at my disposition his family manuscripts, for the illustration of a part of the narrative. So, too, those of General Van Schaick were put in my hands for a similar purpose; some of the most curious of which will be found among the notes.

In revising the original of this work I discovered the marks of haste, but nevertheless I have concluded to leave the text of the work as it was, as artists sometimes do their early productions, their very faults and slips attesting their authenticity. It was prepared for the personal benefit of the narrator, but now that you adopt it as a part of your later publications, I shall secure for it, what it otherwise might not have attained, the advantage of becoming a portion of your valuable series. It has long been out of print, and is only now to be had occasionally by collectors who are ready to pay for it a high price, and one much beyond its value.

The present edition, with some notes and letters never before published, may give it more consideration than it had before.

Yours very truly,

S. DE WITT BLOODGOOD.

NEW YORK, Sept. 1, 1865.

THE SEXAGENARY.

CHAPTER I.

I AM aware of the difficulties which beset the author of a personal narrative. His opinions are almost always tinged with prejudice, and his sketches often distinguished by their mannerism. His efforts, be they ever so well intended, contribute rather to the gratification of individual taste than to the benefit of science at large. But as a vast proportion of readers prefer amusement to philosophy, the autobiographer escapes from the charge of being uninstructive, if he contrives to make his story interesting. Since I first determined to publish these reminiscences I have taken some pains to learn the character of this species of authorship. I stumbled, as it were, upon the memoirs of Gibbon, and the reading of his elegant compositions has somewhat damped the ardor of my zeal. But he observes that if " they are sincere, we seldom complain of the misfortunes or prolixity of these personal memoirs." Under this safeguard I shall attempt the humble narrative of a life chiefly spent in the neighborhood of our northern armies. The principal events of the war of independence are well known, and their happy conclusion has made us justly proud of that remarkable era. Yet who does not regret that so few of the actors on that busy stage have left behind them the written records of their various fortunes? We have now but a little company left of all those heroic battalia. One by one the leaders in the cabinet and the warriors of the field desert the scenes of their renown. What a rich treat would even the "trivial fond records" of their personal history afford to those who seek to rescue their motives, their actions and their characters from the biting tooth of time! The memoirs of some of those sagacious old men who formed our committees of safety, the correspondence of the most intelligent of the Whigs of our own state, would be rich in those incidents by which we judge of men and things, now rapidly vanishing from the view. Such details every reflecting mind would relish; for what are the events of life, the epochs of history, and the annals of nations, but exhibitions of the powers of the human mind displayed in the multifarious forms of its own strange embodying? These are the gems of its casket, or the poison of its laboratory.

Biography, however, which is to history what groups are to the canvass, is more directly addressed to our individual sympathy, since it narrows the view of the observer to some particular point, and appeals to every class and condition, by the presentment of some trait, some resemblance which becomes the more striking, the more irresistible, as it conforms to circumstances which have befallen ourselves.

It was the opinion of Dr. Johnson that there has rarely passed a life, of which a judicious and faithful narrative would be without advantage. It was he who also asserted that the motives of great or little actions were founded alike in the depths of the human heart; upon this principle, the biography of the humblest individual might be fraught with as much advantage to mankind, as that of the high born, the beautiful and brave. "The prince," said he, "who loses his empire, feels no more indignation in proportion to his consequence, than the luckless farmer, at the wretch who steals his cow."

Fortified by authority so respectable, and more than all induced by the cares of poverty which now press upon me with a weight unfelt in happier years, I have at the instance of a gentleman, who has befriended me in adversity, consented to entrust to his hands, the incidents of my life for publication.

Old age is garrulous, but the grain of wheat often lurks in the bushel of chaff, and a piping voice, be it never so musical, may convey a lesson replete with the wisdom of experience.

I am by no means a veteran — I never was in actual combat, but I can shoulder my crutch, exulting at the remembrance of the fight, and show how fields were won. I was neither continental, nor levy. I served in the unpretending, but not useless character of a wagoner, in the quarter master's department, at one time actively employed in forwarding cannon, and laboring with my own horses; at another carrying the relief which saved a post. My station in life was that of a farmer in respectable circumstances, and rather above that which furnished the usual recruits for the regular army. In the course of numerous journeys, I had the opportunity of seeing and hearing much more than if I had been a common soldier. I shall confine myself principally to those incidents which I witnessed, or which were naturally the subject of conversation among my own connections. My view of things may be somewhat novel on this account. Many persons at the present day would be pleased to know, and, if possible, to realize the feelings and reflections of even ordinary individuals during our revolution. We are familiar with the contemplation of the brilliant achievements of our distinguished officers. We scarcely admire any other scenes than those dignified by the presence of our heroes and sages. We gaze on them as on a splendid panorama, over which we follow with delight the lights and shades of the great events in which they bore a part. We watch with admiration the processions of pomp and circumstance in which they figure, as they glide over the scene. On the other hand, of the details, the secret springs, the characters of the humble assistants of the machinery, we are too often left in ignorance. I propose, therefore, to show, in the instance of my own household, how we bore our share of the troubles of the times, how they affected our comfort, or disturbed our repose. Thousands, like my own father and his family, suffered and lamented, rejoiced and exulted, unknown to any beyond their immediate neighborhood, yet doing their duty zealously and faithfully in their proper spheres. If the illustration of such principles, and the examples of such persons are worthy of a place in the corner of my readers' memories; if amid the splendid achievements of art, of education, and of commerce, now dazzling our eyes, a recurrence to other days shall not prove tedious or obtrusive — pardon an old man's garrulity and read on.

2

CHAPTER II.

I AM fast losing my claim to the title I have assumed at the head of this reminiscence. In four years more I shall have reached the age of three score and ten. I was born in Schoharie, and my father was a farmer in independent circumstances, at least for those days. The fields he tilled were his only patrimony, and he found them still rich and fertile, as they were represented to have been when cultivated by his ancestors. The year of my birth was that of the introduction of the stamp act. What advantage a piece of paper possessed, because it bore certain marks upon it, more than any other piece without them, seemed quite a problem with the honest yeomanry of the day. This absurdity, as it appeared, roused the spirit of the people, and though the population of the province was only 90,000, yet their resentment rose to a pitch of violence quite disproportioned to the actual means of resistance. My father often told me that I had commenced my career in a stormy period, and that the unsettled state of the times would probably have an injurious effect upon my prospects, as well as the means of advancement of every young man of my age. And so I have found it. The opportunities of mental improvement were almost of necessity denied to us. Newspapers we had none, and the simplest compilations of grammar and arithmetic were scarce and almost unattainable. When I now contemplate the paternal care of the state, extended to its numerous youth, and its noble appropriations to sustain the cause of education, I feel at what a vast distance the young men of my time were from such enviable advantages. The whole country was disturbed, and continued so until after the revolution. The introduction of the stamp paper seemed to be the signal of disorder. The bells were tolled throughout the states. The mobs were violent. My father often spoke of them, and I heard him say that even Lieut. Govenor Colden's life had been threatened at New York; that his stable was broken into and his carriage carried off and burned is well known. A gentleman's residence, called Vauxhall, was rifled and destroyed, and many valuable articles of a tasteful and scientific character, the laborious collection of years, were made into a bonfire and burned, upon the bare presumption that the owner, Major James, was in favor of the obnoxious law. It is scarcely possible for this generation to understand the state of feeling prevalent at this time. I will assert what I believe is now little known, that many of our most wealthy and influential Whigs were at the bottom of these disorders. The colonial journals of that year will show an active hostility to the government, that became at length too strong for the arm of colonial authority.

After the Earl of Loudon had resigned to General Abercrombie the command of the army which had reduced Oswego, my father, then a young man, was called to Schenectady, by sudden business. He drove his own horses before his own wagon. That place was then fortified. It had the shape of a parallelogram, with two gates, one opening to the eastern, and the other to the northern road, and was garrisoned by about 50 or 60 soldiers. It was planned by Philip Verplank, an engineer, in the year 1755, and for his services at this post, Albany and Redhook, where also there was a battery, he received thirty pounds currency. The substantial look of my father's farm equipage engaged the attention of a wagon master, who, without any ceremony, pressed him into the service. Instead of returning home he was compelled to proceed to Albany, where a load was placed upon his wagon, and he was directed to take up his line of march for the north. The army stores were then deposited in the warehouse of Mr. Ten Eyck, and the load he was compelled to take consisted of dry goods that were wanted at Fort Edward. A large number of persons was engaged in the same business; most of them against their wishes and interests. The train of wagons was urged forward, and the celebrated Colonel Bradstreet had charge and direction of the convoy. At this time General Abercrombie was preparing for an attack on Ticonderoga, with an army superior to any that had ever taken the field in North America. My father told me, that though unwilling to be employed in other people's business to the injury of his own, he was anxious to be present at the expected battle. In order to accomplish his purpose he turned his horse loose into the fields, and took the place of a provincial soldier, in a company to which was attached Lieut. Van Schaick, of Albany, afterwards colonel in the continental service. The circumstance, from its novelty, attracted the attention of the officer commanding the wagon corps, and he interfered to prevent his design, upon the plea that the army did not want soldiers so much as it did wagoners. Foiled in this attempt, he still resolved to go down to the lake with the troops, to witness the attack, and, the better to escape detection, he stole off to a party of Indians, assumed the dress of a warrior, and so well disguised his person, as to be undistinguished from the savages themselves. This attempt also leaked out, and came to the ears of Col. Bradstreet, who went among the Indians to detect the delinquent. This was impossible, for the Indians were too much pleased with such a compliment to their fashions in dress and warfare to betray the young volunteer. The colonel then addressed the savages, and said that he knew that the young man from Schoharie was amongst them, and, unless he threw off his disguise and returned to his duty, he would sequester his wagon and horses, and deprive him of his pay for his services. My father, who had no idea that his freak would draw upon him such consequences as these, stepped out of the group, much to his own mortification, amid roars of laughter from his companions, who began to strip him of his blankets and feathers. Even the savages joined in the laugh against him, as he stood before them, like the daw stripped of his borrowed plumage.

CHAPTER III.

My father had no reason to regret the interference of Col. Bradstreet. He escaped much personal danger by being thwarted in his designs. The complete discomfiture of the army followed the attempt on Ticonderoga. Gen. James Abercrombie[1] seemed incapable of command. If I mistake not, he had seen service in the West Indies, and until his defeat was thought to have been an able officer. The death of Lord Howe, whose fine personal appearance my father often described to me, occurred in this unfortunate battle. His body was brought down to Albany by his sorrowing friends, and deposited under or near the pulpit of the English church. A monument to his memory was erected in Westminster Abbey, at the expense of the colony of Massachusetts.

When the army fell back to its former position, at the head of Lake George, the wagoners were

[1] It has been quite a common error, to consider the General Abercrombie of our early historians the same person who was mortally wounded at Alexandria. The only account we have seen of the personage referred to here, is in the late American edition of Lempriere's *Universal Biography*. Mrs. Grant, in her *Memoirs*, alludes to him very favorably.

ordered to return to the city. I have already mentioned that my father's horses, like the rest, had
been turned out to forage for themselves — regular
supplies of hay and grain were out of the question.
It was, as may be presumed, no easy matter to find
them again. Some of them indeed were never
found, while others were discovered at a distance
of many miles on their way homewards. This gives
a slight idea of the confusion attending the movements of armies on similar occasions.

The main body of wagoners returned by the
west side of the river, but my father and his friends
kept on the east side, and when they reached the
Batten kil, which empties into it, they discovered,
on crossing the bed of the creek, the wet print of
a mocasin upon one of the rocks. They were confident from this circumstance that hostile Indians
were near them, and that one must have passed
that way but a few minutes before. To go back
seemed as dangerous as to go forward. They therefore pushed on towards the river, but had scarcely
reached its bank when the distinct report of a
musket in their rear brought with it the confirma-
tion of their danger.

I should have mentioned, however, that a small
escort was marching down the west side of the
river opposite, to protect the wagoners that had gone

home in that direction. When this firing was heard, therefore, a detachment immediately came across to ascertain the cause. They were not unsuccessful. In a garden belonging to a Mr. De Ruyter the body of a dead man was found, which was still warm. His scalp had been taken off, and, from appearances, he seemed to have been shot while in the act of stooping to weed one of the beds. This established the alarming fact, that the savages in alliance with the French had boldly extended their incursions within the line of the English posts.

It was the fashion in those days, as it has been since, to make as much money as possible out of the public. My father related one incident which, though trifling in itself, elucidates my meaning. One Dirk Van J—e, who had accompanied the army to Lake George, after turning out his horses, pretended that they were lost, and went off ostensibly to look for them. Instead of doing this he secretly departed for Schoharie, where he lived, and when the time was nearly out for which he engaged himself, he returned to head quarters without being suspected, and received the full amount of his stipulated wages. The wagoners were usually very indifferent to the fate of their horses, particularly if they were not of the best kind. The government paid very well for losses of this sort,

although the colonial assembly was far from following the example, in cases where they had raised
levies, or received the assistance of laborers or
farmers, by virtue of the government press war-
rants.   If a horse was found with his throat cut or
his skull cloven by the tomahawk, the owners with
great philosophy received the compensation provided for such casualties, and went home quite
reconciled to their *misfortune.*   An amusing instance
of their general dislike to the service was observed
when Col. Bradstreet mustered the wagoners on
their return from the lake.   He thanked them for
their fidelity and services, and gave them notice he
should want their further aid in forwarding troops
to the Mohawk river, on their way to Fort Stanwix.
An expedition against Oswego being contemplated,
the hint was not lost upon those interested.   The
principal part of them drove their wagons into the
pine bush behind the fort, unharnessed their horses,
and rode off in the night to their respective
homes.   The discovery was not made until the
ensuing morning, and it so effectually disconcerted
the colonel that he discharged the few who remained
without any ceremony.

My father returned home, and saw nothing further, which I recollect to have heard him speak of,
until the following year, when he was called into

service as a militiaman, and proceeded as far west as Fort Stanwix. The losses of the English had so animated the enemy as to bring them into the neighborhood of the Mohawk country. On his return home the party with which he was descending the river was fired upon by the Indians, in the neighborhood of Fort Plain. Fortunately for the attacked, it was a wet day, and the savages had great difficulty in discharging their pieces. The bateaumen were not slow in perceiving this, and with redoubled efforts soon pulled away out of reach of their fire. The subsequent successes of Sir Jeffrey Amherst relieved the inhabitants of the province from further inquietude. My father, to better his situation, removed to the neighborhood of Saratoga, and there he remained pursuing his agricultural avocations for several years, until the approach of more troublesome times.

CHAPTER IV.

THE first intelligence which gave alarm to our neighborhood, and indicated the breaking asunder of the ties which bound the colonies to the mother country, reached us on a Sunday morning. We attended at divine service that day at Schuyler's Flats. I well remember, notwithstanding my youth, the impressive manner with which, in my hearing, my father told my uncle, that BLOOD *had been* SHED *at Lexington.* The startling intelligence spread like fire among the congregation. The preacher was listened to with very little attention. After the morning discourse was finished, and the people were dismissed, we gathered about Gen. Philip Schuyler for further information. He was the oracle of our neighborhood. We looked up to him with a feeling of respect and affection. His popularity was unbounded; his views upon all subjects were considered sound, and his anticipations almost prophetic. On this occasion he confirmed the intelligence already received, and expressed his belief that an important crisis had arrived which must sever us forever from the parent country.

I remember afterwards hearing my father remark, that among the most influential and the best educated part of the community great anxiety was felt as to the termination of the struggle, for a conviction seemed to prevail, that we were unable to sustain ourselves against the armies and navies of England, if brought to bear together and with promptness. I have also heard, that among the unenlightened and uneducated portion of the public, an undoubted apathy in relation to the contest prevailed.

The most common topics of complaint were, that the colonies were taxed as well beyond the necessity of the times, as their ability to pay, and the belief that individuals might be carried to England to be tried for criminal offences, although it was not attended, generally, by the fear of any such occurrence. Very soon, however, the militia began to organize in every part of the country. Our own neighborhood, like others, was divided into districts, and these into beats of companies, and though we did not see any of the display, we saw much of the inconvenience of war. The people of our vicinity assembled together at Batten kil, and as the companies chose their own officers, it so happened that a Mr. T — t and my father were respectively named by their friends for the office of captain. The latter was elected almost unanimously, but he modestly declined the appointment, alleging his want of education and experience for a station involving so much responsibility. He proposed a Mr. Lake, as every way fit for the station ; and as he possessed one great advantage over Mr. T., in being entirely free from all suspicion of being disaffected, he was elected by a large majority. Mr. Lake had also great resolution and presence of mind, and was a man of unspotted character. The militia being in some measure organized, began to be exercised in the use of arms, and those persons who had seen service in the French war were particularly engaged in giving instruction and advice. The drum and fife resounded on all sides, and persons of reflection began to consider the consequences that would follow an appeal to arms.

CHAPTER V.

THE blood shed in the neighborhood of Boston, which in those days seemed to be the centre of motion and conferred its name on every thing connected with our colonial resistance, gave a new impulse to our cause. Arnold, who commenced his career as a captain of a volunteer company in New Haven, proposed to the Massachusetts committee of safety to proceed and capture Ticonderoga and Crown Point. His offer was accepted, and success crowned his efforts. During the French wars Crown Point or Fort St. Frederick was considered the most formidable post— during the revolution Ticonderoga was the most so. Crown Point has been so often described by modern tourists, that it would be quite useless in me to attempt a description, and yet I may say that there are some peculiarities about its former appearance, not so generally known. It was a very strong fort, built of stone, with four bastions, a dry ditch, and a covered way to the lake. In the north-west corner of the fort stood the citadel, also built of stone, and in shape an octagon, four stories in height. This was erected on arches, and was mounted with 20 pieces of cannon. Around this was also a dry ditch, and the entrance was secured by a draw bridge. Its walls were ten feet thick, and the roof was shingled. The fort also contained a chapel, and several wooden buildings. In 1755 the French had put it in complete repair. In 1775 it was quite defenceless, and was supplied with but one sergeant and twelve men, and easily fell before the enterprise of Colonel Warner, the comrade of Arnold.

In the fall of that year my father went up to the north for some loading, consisting of the spoils of the enemy, taken by these gallant officers. He took me with him, and he drove one wagon, while I had charge of the other. On our return a Frenchman and two Indians were placed under our care. They had been taken prisoners, and for some purpose or other were sent down to Albany. The Indians were very sulky. They did not or could not speak the English language, and appeared unwilling to make the attempt. The Frenchman claims a place in my memory, from being one of the lowest class of *habitans*, as well as the filthiest. At a place now called Washington we lodged on our way down, and the Frenchman soon fell asleep before the fire. In the progress of his " nid, nid, nodding," his hat fell off and displayed to our view countless myriads of nameless animals. The Indians seemed as much

astonished as ourselves, and broke into loud grunt-
ings at the disgusting sight. I mention the circumstance chiefly for the purpose of stating, that savages are in this particular very cleanly, and to show
that the extremes of civilization and barbarism very
often meet. The inn-keeper vented his undisguised
rage at the Canadian, and told him with many impre-
cations that it was lucky for him he was a prisoner.

Our loading consisted of British military camp
equipage, pans, flints, and other articles, which, together with the post from which they came, had been
captured in behalf of the "Lord and the continental
congress."

The weather was cold and disagreeable, the roads
were bad, and the whole business to me vexatious.
A luckless urchin I considered myself, to be thus
perched on top of a wagon, jolted to death, with
the air penetrating to my very vitals. Yet we traveled at the rate of twenty miles a day, and after
bestowing our cargo at Albany, we turned our faces
towards Saratoga and our own firesides. Ere we
arrived a snow storm commenced, and covered the
ground to the depth of several inches.

I had forgotten to mention that a small detach-
ment of continentals accompanied us down from
Fort George, a post which was designed by Col.
Montresor, and called his Folly. I shall not in this

place describe it; but of the garrison, of which this detachment had been a part, I would mention that they were downright oddities. Their blue coats with white facings were tarnished by the smoke of the pine knots, which it was the fashion in Fort George to use in the double capacity of fire and candle. A more sombre family I think I never saw.

We were not, however, permitted to enjoy our homes. My father having a good share of the patronage, as well as confidence of the leading men in our neighborhood, with a snug property of his own and a good number of horses, was very much in demand when any urgent and rapid movement of stores and supplies was to be effected. The cannon captured from the enemy were next to be brought down from the north, and as many as one hundred and twenty, besides howitzers and swivels, had fallen into our hands with the two fortresses before mentioned. They had been in part removed to the head of Lake George, and thither we were directed to proceed for them. Col. Knox, afterwards the able chief of our artillery, undertook to superintend their removal in person. He had very heavy sleds prepared for the occasion, and a numerous train set out from our neighborhood to bring down the cannon. We reached Glen's Falls the first night, even then celebrated as an object of curiosity.

CHAPTER VI

LONG before daylight we were on the move. I had trouble of managing an extra pair of horses. We had taken on many more than the usual number in consequence of the service in which we were engaged. My father was some distance in the rear, while by accident I was considerably in advance of him. The road was dreary, the darkness great, and I anything but comfortable during the morning drive. We were approaching the bloody pond and the scene of some terrible slaughters. My imagination peopled every bush with ghosts. In this pond hundreds of those slain in the battles between Sir William Johnson and the French Baron Dieskau were carelessly thrown, the hurry and distress of the hour permitting no other receptacle for the dead. My nervous excitement increased every instant. I anxiously turned my ear to listen to the sounds of the voices behind me, which came along in melancholy intervals, and would then be lost for apparently an interminable period. While I was thus in spite of myself giving way to the most unpleasant feelings, my leading horses, which had been jogging along on a pace quite inconsistent with my views of propriety, made a sudden halt and fell back upon the pair next the sled. This sudden stop only increased my confusion. I could not help thinking that the animals saw something which I could not. I remembered an old superstition that *dogs can see ghosts*, and I now fancied that horses might have the same facility. I did not, however, forget myself. I made a most rapid and liberal use of my whip, when, with first a recoil, then a plunge and a desperate scramble, the horses leaped over something which seemed to be in their way, and went on at full gallop for some distance. I at length succeeded in arresting their flight and began to bawl lustily to those who were far away in the rear. After making the woods resound with my halloos, I had the satisfaction of hearing a reply. My father came swiftly up, when I informed him of what had occurred. A diligent search was then made along the roads by the persons in our company. What should the cause of my anxiety prove to be, but a drunken soldier, who had, in some unaccountable way, fallen asleep on the road, overcome by fatigue and intoxication. We discovered no very great injury on his person, and we carried him with us to Fort George, where he was taken care of by his comrades. From that time I never saw him more.

This occurrence drew forth several interesting anecdotes, in relation to the conflicts which had taken place in the neighborhood, and as I have not seen them in any of our histories, I will venture to give them a place, with the remark that they were received as authentic at the time.

Dieskau was rather an old man; he was wounded in his legs and both his hips. He was brought to Sir William Johnson's tent at about six o'clock in the evening, just at the moment as that officer had his wound dressed, caused by a bullet lodged in his thigh.

The French commander, it was said, brought his troops up in a very imposing manner, with bayonets fixed and glittering, and continued the engagement with a firmness that made Sir Willam's troops often waver. But a very expert gunner, Mr. Boyle, threw some shell and 32 lb. shot among the Frenchmen, which made them at length give way. This retrieved the fortunes of the day. The Mohawk Indians lost their great chief, King Hendrik, in the early part of the day, and took an unusual number of scalps in consequence — eighty were brought in after the engagement. Hendrik was killed in the first of the conflicts, and when his son was informed of his being slain he gave a loud groan, and then placing his hand on his heart exclaimed, Ah, ha! *Hendrik alive here yet!* A report prevailed very currently among the provincials that the French soldiers chewed the balls which they used on this occasion, because when extracted they had a green color, and were very ragged. Baron Dieskau, on being told of this, said that if such was the case it was entirely without his knowledge, and that he was sure none of the veterans he had brought with him from Europe would be guilty of conduct so unsoldierlike. This person recovered partially of his wounds, was taken to England, and there died.

Our business, as I have already mentioned, was to transport the captured artillery. It was a seasonable supply, and we felt an unusual degree of interest in fulfilling our contracts. The pieces were apportioned to our respective companies. My father took in charge a heavy iron nine pounder, which required the united efforts of four horses to drag it along. Others had the heavy resistance of 18s and 24s to overcome, which required the exertions of at least eight horses. We had altogether about forty or fifty pieces to transport, and our cavalcade was quite imposing. We traveled back towards Albany without accident, until we reached Lansing's ferry, on the Hudson. As the ice was not uncommonly strong some precautions were taken to get across with safety. The method

adopted was this : A rope forty feet long was fastened to the tongue of the sleigh, and the other end
was attached to the horses. The first gun was
started across in this way, and my father walked
along aside the horses with a sharp hatchet in his
hand, to cut the rope, if the cannon and sled should
break through.   In the centre of the river the ice
gave way, as had been feared, and a noble 18 sank
with a crackling noise, and then a heavy plunge to
the bottom of the stream.   With a desperate hope
of overcoming its downward tendency, and just as
the cracking of the ice gave the alarm, the horses
were whipped up into a full jump, but to no purpose.

The gun sank, fortunately, not in very deep
water. The horses kept their feet, and the rope
was used to secure a buoy over the place where the
cannon was lying, and afterwards materially aided
its recovery.   In this dilemma we had no alternative but to abandon the idea of getting on the east
side of the Hudson.   It began to rain, the weather
was changing, and we were forced to retrace our
steps in some measure, and seek a passage across
the Mohawk. We reached the ferry of Mr. Claus
the same day, and crossed in safety.   The next day
we entered Albany.   Our appearance excited the
attention of the burghers.   They were accustomed,

it is true, to seeing fine artillery, as some well
appointed armies had been encamped within the
city. But this was the first artillery which congress had been able to call their own, and it led to
reflections not in the least injurious to our cause.

CHAPTER VII.

THE weather now became colder, and we crossed at the south ferry, without difficulty, or even apprehension. Some of the party here bought out, from some of their friends, the right, as they termed it, of carrying over the eighteen pounders, and it was considered a good speculation. We received for drawing such, one and four pence a mile, and when we were detained by breakages or other accidents, and laid by for repair, we received 15 shillings a day. As we reached the shore at Greenbush, a tongue of one of the sleds, which was loaded with a smaller gun, struck and perforated the side of a very handsome pleasure boat, and made a breach in it of rather a ruinous character. The driver seemed to have no alternative but to keep moving; he drove fairly over it, and the boat was made a complete wreck. The idea that congress would pay all damages was the only sympathy that we had then time to bestow on the owner. Whether congress responded to the sentiments of our corps we never learned. We made the best of our way to Claverack, and there the breaking down of a sleigh detained us two whole days. The depend-

5

ence we were under to each other for assistance,
in case of accident, made it neccessary for us to
move in a body. We then reached Westfield, Massachusetts, and were much amused with what
seemed the quaintness and honest simplicity of the
people. Our armament here was a great curiosity.
We found that very few, even among the oldest
inhabitants, had ever seen a cannon. They were
never tired of examining our desperate "big shooting irons," and guessing how many tons they
weighed; others of the scientific order were mea-
suring the dimensions of their muzzles, and the
circumference at the breech. The handles, as they
styled the trunnions, were *reckoned* rather too short,
but they considered, on the whole, that the guns
must be pretty nice things at a long shot. We
were great gainers by this curiosity, for while they
were employed in remarking upon our guns,
we were, with equal pleasure, discussing the qualities of their cider and whiskey. These were
generously brought out in great profusion, saying
they would be darned if it was not their treat. One
old mortar, well known during the revolution as
the old sow, and which not many years since was
the subject of eulogy on the floor of our own
legislature, by no less a personage than Gen. Root,
was actually fired several times by the people of

Westfield, for the novel pleasure of listening to its deep toned thunders. Col. Knox was surrounded by visitors at the inn that evening. And the introductions that took place, gave to his acquaintance hosts of militia officers of every rank and degree. Every man seemed to be an officer. What a pity, said Colonel Knox to some of us who stood near him, what a pity it is that our soldiers are not as numerous as our officers. But the happiness of these people was not to last forever. We moved on to Springfield, and they had nothing left but the remembrance of what they had seen, to console them for our departure.

We reached Springfield (the great place of deposit for arms), but could get no further. The sleighing failed, and we had to leave our cannon lying ingloriously on the road side, in the mud. I cannot give any further account of their travels. I believe they afterwards were not without effect in various bloody fights, and from having been intended by their first owners as the *ultima ratio regum*, they settled down on their beds the plain and forcible advocates of the doctrines of the continental congress. We returned to Albany in much quicker time than it took us to get to Springfield. Here our services were again imperiously required by the exigency of our northern affairs. Supplies

were wanted at our northern posts, and among
them strong waters were not an inconsiderable
item. Happy would it be for the world if the use
did not lead to the abuse, and the remedy for human
suffering became not worse than the disease. At
that time, however, I was any thing but a contem-
plator of human affairs in the abstract, and I was
soon seen with a heavy load of the bane of human
kind, following in the train as unconcerned as any
other of my companions. We now took the road
to Montreal. On our way up we availed ourselves
of every opportunity to travel on the ice. We
arrived at Fort George (February, 1776), and
crossed the lake, once so celebrated as Lake St.
Sacrament by Canadian devotees. Its crystal
drops were thought so pure as to be eagerly sent
for by the priests, to be used as holy water, and to
fill the founts employed in their offices of the
sacrament of baptism. We arrived at Ticonderoga,
which presented but a sorry sight; the glories of
Ti were rather on the wane; the fortune of war
and a change of masters had not in the least bene-
fitted its military appearance. Its ditches were
nearly filled with rubbish, and its ramparts were
dismantled and ruinous. It was here I heard of
the circumstance never yet explained by any of
the numerous journalists and historians who have

filled their pages with its eventful story. I allude to a plate of copper or brass, which was found here on the capture of this post, and was inscribed with these words: "*Pone Principes Eorum Sicut Oreb et Zeb, Zeba et Zalmanna.*" The expression itself is taken from the Psalms of David; but, to whom it was meant to apply, or what precise import was intended to be conveyed by it, is a question yet to be answered. From Ti we proceeded northwardly on the ice. Sixty-two sleighs on this occasion were under the care of my father, and he pushed forward with great diligence. We considered the events of the approaching campaign as probably depending upon our individual efforts. Montreal was in our possession, Quebec closely besieged, and we were impressed with the necessity of doing every thing in our power to keep them in supplies. On our way up we passed an island called Schuyler's Island. It was what in modern times would have been called our bivouac. Our sleighs were all driven together in a row. Our horses were rubbed, fed and blanketed, and tied to the sleighs. We were divided into messes of six men each, and went to work quite systematically to secure ourselves a comfortable night, notwithstanding the snow was three and a half feet deep. We dug it away in different places in the manner of the

Esquimaux, and in our frozen apartments we likened ourselves to lodgers in a lower story. Some diligently collected fuel for the fires, and others stripped the walnut tree of its bark, which to the voyager is so well known in its quick kindling, and for its resemblance to pitch pine. Our bags, containing the oats for our horses, were snugly stowed around our sleeping apartments, which were also made comfortable by a well replenished fire. After eating a hearty supper, which, if not distinguished for its cookery, was well relished for its flavor, we sank on our beds, and soon forgot our troubles and our toils. Had they been of down we could not have slept more sweetly and refreshingly — so strangely do circumstances control our feelings and moderate our desires.

CHAPTER VIII.

W E continued our journey without any very striking incidents, but were glad to pass the next night under a comfortable roof, instead of the canopy of the skies. In the course of the next day several of our sleighs fell through the ice, but they were recovered without loss to their owners. Our rendezvous was the next night at La Cole river, the banks of which have witnessed the pertinacity of a certain stone mill, in later times. We had scarcely made ourselves snug in our quarters before a regiment of Pennsylvania troops overtook us, having traveled in sleighs. Our track in the snow facilitated their progress. They were a long desired reinforcement, with which it was expected to carry Quebec. It was my opinion at the time, which was afterwards justified by the result, that Quebec was not to be taken by such troops. They were the most quarrelsome, and I regret to say, profligate set of men I had ever seen together. They had plenty of money with them and spent it profusely. The vices of insubordination, gambling and rioting, marked their battalia, and we ourselves had great trouble with them, notwith-

standing our pacific character. It was not surprising
that their subsequent behavior in Lower Canada
produced disaffection among the very inhabitants,
on whose friendship our success was chiefly to
depend. Indeed, it is recorded by all the histories
of that campaign, that after the death of Montgomery the conduct of our troops was absolutely
shocking. If they purchased any thing they paid
in certificates, which the quarter master general
rejected for informality, often indeed for the want
of a signature. The houses of the country people
were plundered, their religion was abused. The
inhabitants were fired at as they went to mass. The
priests themselves were robbed, and outrages of
every description were committed. In this way
even the best friends of congress were discouraged,
and it actually became necessary for that body to
pass a resolution in April of that year, ordering our
commissioners to cause justice to be done them,
and to inflict exemplary punishment on those who
violated their military regulations.

But it is a further fact, that even this resolution
was without its effect, notwithstanding the exertions
of that amiable man, Gen. Thomas, the American
commander, who afterwards died of the small pox
while on his return from Quebec. It is also a matter of fact, that the notorious Arnold, whose gallant

conduct in arms seemed to be clouded by a disposition which partook as well of the love of plunder
as the love of glory, carried away with him from
Montreal a large quantity of goods, taken from the
very people that congress had made a show of
protecting.   When he ordered Colonel Hazen to
take charge of them on crossing the river he met
with a decided refusal and an expression of disapprobation.   When General Arnold reached Crown
Point, and found some of his plunder missing, he
was followed by the owners with their accounts,
who demanded payment.   Arnold vented his rage
on Col. Hazen, by having him brought before a
court martial for his neglect of the goods.   Col. H.
was of course honorably acquitted, while Gen. A.
was personally so disrespectful to the court, chal-
lenging the members to fight him, and abusing
them without any justice, that they demanded his
arrest, and nothing but the extreme necessity which
existed of employing his talents on Lake Champlain at that time prevented his disgrace and ruin.
Gen. Gates dissolved the court martial, and Arnold
was made a commander *pro tempore*.   It may
not be amiss to state, that Colonel Hazen, as it
is said, was originally an officer in the British
army, a captain of rangers under Wolfe, and a
favorite officer of that general.   He raised a regi-

ment principally of Canadians, and was an active and useful commander. His widow, Madame Hazen, a French woman, died a few years since in the city of Albany, where she had lived for many years in great privacy. But to return to my narrative; we preceded these turbulent Pennsylvanians in order to keep out of their way, traveling late and early. We next reached St. Johns, and passed a night within the fort. My curiosity being roused, I hastened to examine the works considered almost impregnable, until General Montgomery captured them, about five months previous. He had actually expended all his ammunition before it, without making any impression. And the result would have been very dubious, had not the capture of the fort at Chamblee and the arrival of six tons of excellent powder enabled the American general to push his attack with increased hopes. A battery within two hundred and sixty yards of the fort, mounting four guns and six mortars, was erected under a heavy fire from the garrison. The failure of Sir Guy Carleton to relieve them, the pertinacity of the besiegers and the shortness of the provision of the besieged, compelled Major Preston to surrender. An original note, written during the siege by the aid of General Montgomery, is now in my possession, and is couched in the following language:

" The enemy having discovered our north-west work, are firing upon it. The general therefore, desires you will order the gunners at the east battery to pay attention to the north-west side of the fort. I am, sir, your humble servant,

JOHN M'PHERSON,

Aid-de-Camp."

Although but about twelve years of age, I have, in relation to the capture, a vivid recollection of my inquiries and researches, which, coupled with the infomation of after life, has made an indelible impression on my memory. Arrived at Laprairie, we crossed to Montreal on the ice, and the crossing was difficult and dangerous. The river was frozen in huge waves, over which we had to pitch and plunge along. And I distinctly remember, the story which circulated amongst us at the time was, that there was a premium of fifty pounds given by the government every winter, to the first man who drove over the frozen billows to Laprairie.

My recollections of Montreal are not very flattering to that place, and although I have visited it frequently since, I never saw any thing very prepossessing in its narrow streets and gloomy houses. Our supplies were deposited in a store, and we remained there for four days, during which time I examined every part of the town. Very few of our

troops were then there, and the inhabitants discovered great diversity of feeling on the subject of
the war.   The most, however, were friendly, as was
afterwards proved by their kindness and hospitality
to those poor wretches whom the small pox and
other diseases forced upon their charities, during
the retreat of our troops from Canada.

Before I proceed with my personal narrative I may
be excused for referring to one or two original letters, now before me, which carry back the mind to
the scenes of other days.   Colonel Clinton, afterwards well known in our revolution as a gallant
general officer, and now not less remembered as the
father of the illustrious De Witt Clinton, commanded
a battery at Point Levi.   An original letter from
General Arnold to Colonel Clinton, now before me,
contains these words :

"You will please compleat the battery as soon
as possible, and when it is done to heat shot.   You
will begin firing on the town.   Begin moderately
until you have the distance well.   Let the shot be
well heated.   I think we had best aim at the town
and leave the.shiping for the present.   With your
shot, heave now and then a shell.

B. ARNOLD."

April 1, 1776.

Colonel Clinton afterwards commanded at Montreal, and besides having orders to destroy the towns if the enemy approached, and the inhabitants were hostile, had also instructions from Samuel Chase and Charles Carroll, of Carrolton, which are now before me, in their hand writing, to seize the inhabitants of Montreal as hostages, and send them over to Longueil or Laprairie.

The following is copied verbatim, from the original, written by a Roman catholic priest at Point Levi, during the siege of Quebec:

Domine mi, falsa testimonia contra me sunt facta sed parvi refert. Deus scit me esse innocentum. Rogo te ut placeat tibi hanc epistolam mittere statim ad Dominum Arnold in Castris. Gratias tibi habebo. Vale Bene valeasque doleo propter te quia sis dægrotus. Semper fui sincerus et mihi non videtur justum ferre judicium contra me, qua tantum parte adversa exaudita, me nen audite ullo modo.

BERTHIAUME, PRETRE.

CHAPTER IX.

AT Montreal, where the French language or a corruption of it was universally spoken, I found myself compelled to resort to the universal language of signs. By these and the shrugs, which are as important in the conversation of a Frenchman as his words, I managed to make myself understood. Our continental money required a *good deal of gesticulation to make it go.* It was not much relished by our Canadian friends, at its par value. One of my amusements was to play tricks upon an old market woman, who retailed articles out of a dog cart, still a vehicle in great repute in Canada. Her shrill voice, and exclamations of Vola (voila) mauvay (mauvais) Bostony! still haunt my memory. I mention this to confirm the statement I have often since read, that the Americans were then almost universally called Bostonians in Europe and Canada, and our revolution, now the theme of swelling eulogy, was then known as the "Bostonian affair."

Our business was soon dispatched, and we turned our faces homewards. On our return, a prisoner, Captain Swan, of the British army, and an Irishman, was permitted to go home, on his parole, by the way of New York. We carried him with us. He was a fine looking man, and resembled General Burgoyne. He had been made a prisoner near or at Quebec. An arrangement was entered into for his conveyance as far as Poughkeepsie, and to my father was committed the trust of conducting him there safely. His red coat and laced cocked hat became him, but his manners were reserved and sour. Indeed we were but plain people, and perhaps it was not in our power to have become very agreeable to him, so we did not attempt any thing more than to make him comfortable. He had his son with him, a pert, mischievous boy, seven or eight years of age, who was dressed in regimentals, and had been with him in camp; a servant in undress completed his suite. This latter was an extravagant talker about the country he had left, and dear Erin was the theme of his unaffected praise. Horse racing was his passion, and many fine stories he told us of a celebrated Irish colt called the Potheen mare, which outran every thing in the world. As we were crossing Lake George we met further reinforcements, going on to Montreal. I saw thirty men traveling in one sleigh. Several short planks were placed across the sleigh, and on them the men stood up to catch the stiff breeze blowing from the south. These human sails carried them along at a rapid

rate, and the horses, so far from feeling the weight
behind them, were going at some speed so as not
to be run upon by the sleigh. It had a singular
appearance, but was not without merit in idea and
usefulness in its effect. Capt. Swan was safely taken
to Poughkeepsie, and my father returned home,
where the labors of his farm occupied him for the
remainder of the year. It was distinguished, however, by a most remarkable event, not only worthy
of individual remembrance, but of public eulogy
to the latest times. The declaration of independence — the declaration that we were, and of right
ought to be, free and independent, was published
throughout the country with great rejoicings. It
was read at the head of our brigades, and in this
part of our country casks of liquor were opened,
and liberal potations were made to the " honor and
glory " of the continental congress. At Stillwater
a large collection of people were assembled, as
soon as the news arrived, and General Schuyler
among the number. This patriot and soldier, by
his presence and exertions, contributed not a little
to keep up the glow which was necessary to add
spirit to our sentiments and boldness to our actions.

It may not be amiss to state that it was about
this time that General Sullivan passed down to
Albany from the north, having been superseded by
General Gates. Our army there had suffered much,

and we daily saw its remnants on their way home, worn down with hardships, if not disabled by disease. The general hospital was at Fort George, and upwards of three hundred invalids had from time to time been placed there.

In the fall we heard of the great fire at New York, but we did not regard it so much from the reflection that the enemy, who were in possession of it, would be the chief sufferers. Our time had not yet come. The hardships and calamities of war were not yet brought to our own homes and firesides.

CHAPTER X.

EARLY in the year 1777 my father and I were again in active employment. Large quantities of provisions had been accumulating at Bennington for the use of our northern armies, and the New England people had been quite industrious in furnishing their quota of supplies. It was their fashion in those days to use oxen almost entirely for draught, and horses were scarcely seen among them. The New Yorkers have been always noted for the prevailing use of horses, and the assertion may be hazarded, that at that day, as well as now, they possessed a greater number of these animals than any other state. As there was always some contention about getting a job, as it was called, my father took the precaution to bring the loads contracted for, down to his own farm, and then he carried them to the north afterwards, as he had leisure. We went with them to Whitehall, then known as Skenesborough, the residence of Colonel Skene, a noted tory, whose residence and old stone barn were at this time in the quiet possession of a few troops as a garrison, under the command of Colonel Livingston. We traveled down Lake

George to Ti, and there delivered our loads. On our second trip we had scarcely unloaded our sleighs when Colonel Hay, well known as an active and efficient quarter master general, informed us that we must stay and commence dragging timber for the bridge which was about to be constructed by order of congress between Ti and Mount Independence. The object was to strengthen the posts, and the bridge was a floating structure stretching over between them, and was protected by a boom thrown across the lake below. Above, large caissons were sunk to obstruct the navigation. As we had not yet fulfilled our contract in regard to forwarding the supplies, my father remonstrated, and mentioned that if he was not allowed to bring on the remainder as he had contracted, before the lake opened, it would after that become impracticable. Colonel Hay, however, said that it was far more important for him to assist in the construction of the works than to transport the supplies, although the troops had, for months previously, been living from day to day on precarious and scanty rations. My father, on this occasion, gave a specimen of his boldness and ingenuity, and it illustrated the manner in which every thing was managed in those days. An officer was dispatched to take charge of our party, and my father then requested permission

to cross over to Mount Independence to deposit his
load.   He gave me private instructions to follow
him at all hazards.   The officer jumped into my
sleigh and stood up in it.   My father led the way,
and drove down hill at full speed in another direction than the one intended.   I followed him as fast
as possible, when the officer cried out, where are
you going to ?   I replied, after my father, and a
fresh application of the whip made the horses dash
on in the most furious manner.   The officer in full
dress, and not relishing the strange manœuvre, nor
even understanding it, thought proper to jump out
of the sleigh, and in doing so, described a parabolic
curve, or rather a long ellipse, which gave him
time to turn heels upward, and descended with
velocity, head foremost in the snow.   I gave him
one look over my shoulder as he was flying through
the air, and then another, when I perceived him
stuck upright in the snow, like a guide board, one
foot pointing to Mount Independence, and the
other to Ti.   But I was too happy at the thought
of again rejoining my father to indulge in any
other sentiments than those of exceeding joy.

We very soon got under the brow of the hill,
and on the lake shore, where, to our surprise, we
found many others of our companions before us,
parleying with a sentry, who guarded the roads to

the lake, and who required them to show a permit before he could allow them to pass. It was a critical moment for us, as we expected an alarm and pursuit. One John Mahony, a neighbor of ours, had previouly drawn out of his pocket an old certificate, and though unable to read himself, endeavored from memory to mutter out the words of a permit. Nor was the sentry any wiser, for he could not read, and Mahony had declared that it was a pass for nine sleighs, the exact number that was already there, before we arrived. My father, with great presence of mind corrected him, and read the paper so it appeared a permit for eleven sleighs. The sentry took all for granted as he saw the paper before his eyes, and we came off together in high glee. We were then safe, for however within the line of sentinels we were liable to detention, beyond them we knew we were not to be overtaken either by their fire or by pursuit on any of the worn out horses of the garrison.

Some others of our companions were not so fortunate. Coming down the wrong road, with similar intentions of escaping from impressment, like that which my father had determined not to submit to, they crossed the very same sentinel, though under circumstances which showed confusion at seeing him : still they determined to force their

way past him. He hailed them. They pretended
not to hear him. He hailed again. They were
deaf. He hailed again. They kept their horses
at full speed. The sentinel fired, and as they were
exactly in range of his fire the ball struck the
nearest sleigh, passed between the legs of the
driver, between the horses in front, and struck
the next sleigh, where it lodged. They were out
of reach before he could fire again. The occurrence
was one of notoriety at the time, and we all saw
the marks of the sentinel's intentions. When we
arrived at Fort Anne we had another similar attempt at coercion to resist. A sentinel there also
stopped us, and we were ordered to remain and to
load with hides, to be carried down to Albany for
the purpose of being manufactured into shoes for
the army. As it was getting late in the season, and
we were anxious to finish our contract before it was
impracticable, objections were made to going on to
Albany at that time. Mahony endeavored to force
the guard, but a scuffle took place, and he was overpowered. An officer came up, and as he was in-
clined to use compulsion, we hit upon the expedient
of giving one of our companions, an honest, good
natured milita officer, the title of colonel; and, in a
measure, placed ourselves under his protection.
William Van W., although acting in a capacity not

very military at the time, was a respectable man,
infinitely more so than hundreds who had obtained
rank in our continental and militia service, notwithstanding their total incapacity, moral and intellect-
ual. The mention of his title had considerable
effect upon the press-gang. By mutual agreement,
a further arrangement was to be made in relation
to the business, at the fort, which was on a piece of
rising ground. The sentinel himself, far from being
boisterous, civilly pointed at the road which went
across the creek and round a point of land, while
he took a short cut across the point to be there as
soon as we. The colonel forgot his rank and his
promise, and so did we. The moment we were out
of view, under the rise of ground, we left the officer
to imagine what he pleased. We drove off towards
home at full speed, and were soon out of his reach.
These circumstances are related with some minute-
ness, in order to give a faithful picture of the time.

CHAPTER XI.

THIS post was in fact a mere block-house surrounded by palisades. It was near the creek, which poured down the rocks into the basin below, and in its passage turned the wheel of a saw-mill. We escaped from the block-house and its occupants, and reached our home without further molestation. We took up our last load, and again set out for Ticonderoga, which we reached without incident. But when we arrived there some apology was indispensible for our previous conduct. My father, albeit unused to play the orator, acted as spokesman for the delinquents. As I have a full recollection of the interview with Colonel Hay, I will give the particulars. Wiping his forehead with the back of his hand, handkerchiefs being rather scarce in those days, and then straightening his locks over his forehead, he gave a hem, and a nod, and then observed briefly, and to the point, "Well, here we are again, Colonel Hay." "Yes, so I perceive," said the colonel, "and the public interests have suffered severely by your late conduct. I must hold you responsible for the consequences." My father instantly replied: "I have no objections to be held responsible, my urgent business is now finished. My word is kept, my contract is finished. You can take any course the *law* will *warrant*." Colonel Hay knew his man. He immediately observed, "Give me your word that the sleighs in your company shall remain to assist us for a few days, and I am satisfied." My father did not hesitate to give the required promise, as he was always willing to aid the service, and he well knew the necessity of completing the works of defence, then in a state of preparation, to resist the approaching enemy.

The great bridge was not yet finished, and on the morrow and three successive days our whole party was most assiduously employed in drawing timber. It was a bridge of communication, built of wood, which was supported by twenty-two sunken pieces of large timber at nearly equal distances. The spaces between them were filled by separate floats, each fifty feet long and twelve wide, strongly fastened by chains and bolts, and affixed to the sunken piers. In front of this was a boom made of large round pieces of timber, secured by riveted bolts and double chains of inch and a half iron. It was a strong work.

The rapid change of the weather soon rendered our sleighs awhile useless, and our return home necessary. My father was again the organ of communication, and Colonel Hay agreed to discharge the whole party if three pairs of horses could be purchased at fair prices for the service. My father readily undertook to obtain them, and a general muster of all our cattle immediately took place. The object was then explained, and, as he had from the first anticipated, *all were willing to sell.* The three pairs were selected with sleighs and harness. The highest price paid was two hundred and seventy dollars. The money was counted out to them from a store of continental currency that afterwards gave great comfort to the officers of Burgoyne's army as they traveled through New England, particularly those old campaigners who had anticipated some such exigency as that which made them the guests rather than the masters of the people they had expected to subjugate. The purchase being thus effected, we came away, right glad to be released from the laborious operation of dragging over hill and dale the immense pieces of timber which were to become integral parts of the defence of Ticonderoga.

I remember that as our provisions grew scarce during this period of our probation, we were served with the same food which was dealt out to the garrison. My organs of digestion were not quite equal to the task imposed upon them by our new diet. I became most deplorably sick, and often wished myself home that I might share in the daily comforts of a well stocked larder and cleanly board. I really thought my last hour was come. "Brandy and burnt sugar" were scarcely a palliative. But "Time and the hour run through the roughest day," and I recovered almost as expeditiously as I became indisposed. The detention of a few days was not regretted by those who had occasion for the services of our party. At length we sat out for Skenesboro', and there fresh trouble awaited us. The commanding officer remembered the trick we played him, but had not ventured to interrupt us on our way north, loaded as we were with important supplies for Ticonderoga. Now, however, a sergeant and file of men took possession of our "pale caravan." We were compelled by the law of the strongest to go to work drawing sawlogs for the confounded little sawmill I have before mentioned. Here we tugged away in no good humor for several days, when my father's generalship again brought us off with *flying* colors.

CHAPTER XII.

THE escape from our new tormentors was brought about in the following manner. A day was fixed on which to make the attempt. On that day I was told by my father to take charge of the pair of horses I had usually under my care, and lead them into the woods, where, in a certain place, covered up with branches of wood, I would find my sleigh, and that done to follow, by a given route, the party who were to take an early start. I did so, leading one horse and riding the other, under the excuse that I was well enough now to go to the woods. When I reached the forest I could not at first discover the place where our sleigh was concealed. I looked and looked in vain. Every moment I feared the long absence of the company would lead to inquiry and detection. They were well all gone, and I was left alone to bear, perhaps, the weight of increased resentment. My father gone too! The idea was absolutely frightful. Overcome by the most pain-ful recollections I sobbed, I wept aloud. In the moment of this anguish my eyes caught a glimpse of the place of concealment. My tears ceased to flow. I moved off at a brisk pace to the spot, and found the object of my search. It was but a minute's work to adjust the harness. It took but another to get my horses at full speed. I drove them for eight miles as fast as they would go, and a joyful meeting it was when I overtook my friends. They had left me behind for the purpose of making good their retreat, well knowing that if I had been detected my youth would have saved me from any difficulties, and have prevented my detention. My escape, however, was foremost in my own mind, and I considered myself almost a hero, in consequence of the adventure.

It formed the subject of an animated description to my mother, when I once more came within the purview of her domestic circle, and home was never more agreeable to me than when I reached it at this time.

It was generally understood that Ticonderoga would have held out against the enemy. But St. Clair had under his command only a force of three or four hundred men, not all effective, and was not very well supplied with the means of subsisting them. This able and patriotic individual, after serving under Wolfe, and gaining a high character for his military services, even as a subaltern, obeyed the call of his country at the very commencement

of the revolution, and abandoned affluence, a happy
and interesting family, and the charms of Ligonier
valley, to serve the cause of freedom and of man.
At the battle of Trenton he had contributed essen-
tially to the glory and success of that enterprise,
and is even said to have originated it.

Unfortunately for him, as the event proved, he
was selected to oppose an army which Burgoyne
was leading on, flushed with the victories it had
achieved in the old world. The loss of the American flotilla on Lake Champlain increased the difficulty of his position, and he found himself unable
to maintain a post requiring a force much larger
than he possessed. Under all these embarrassing
circumstances the enemy approached — they expected a bloody fight, but at the same time were
prepared to open on Ti from the higher ground on
Sugar Hill, a fire which would have made its further
defence impracticable. The celebrated evacuation
of the post followed, and through the indiscretion
of General Fermoy, who set fire to his dwelling,
the enemy had sufficient light thrown on the movements of St. Clair to make instant preparation for
pursuit. The result, however, set the whole country in confusion, and we now began to look forward
to scenes of distress and suffering.

My father had succeeded this season in raising

the finest crops on his farm he ever had. His
wheat and rye were abundant, and in fine order.
He now began to think, as the rumors of Burgoyne's
approach increased, that he had raised them for the
use of the enemy. The news of our losses at Ticonderoga and Hubbardton had spread like wild
fire among all classes, and we expected nothing else
than the rapid approach of Sir John, as he was
then called.

In the bitterness of disappointment the unfortunate St. Clair received a full share of denunciation,
and we forgot that he had saved an army, which
was far more important to us than a post. All im-
partial observers have acquitted him of blame; but
the justice of his country never restored him to the
situation in which it found him, when it first
demanded his services. Abandoned to poverty and
neglect, the veteran lingered out a wretched existence, forgotten by the young and fiery politicians
of later times, whose only object seems too much
to consist in gratifying the lust of office. This may
seem a harsh judgment, but the feelings of an old
man, who knows what sacrifices were made in the
times that tried men's souls, must be an apology
for the expression of his indignation at the policy
of later periods.

General St. Clair, with the remnants of his force,

joined General Schuyler at Fort Edward, who, on this occasion, as every other, was firm, cool, resolute and undismayed. My father was in the habit of familiar intercourse with him, and being a member of the committee of safety was often on the most confidential terms. I cannot avoid here again paying my feeble tribute to the memory of this good and great man. I will not enter into an account of his military character; it would be unnecessary at this time, when ample justice is done him by his countrymen. But I can say of him, what it gives me pleasure to assert, that he was the idol of the inhabitants of Saratoga. He was looked upon as a sound, judicious man, patriot a and a statesman, and one whose influence had a most salutary effect at this crisis of our northern campaign. During this time, while he was at the north, I remember a simple present was sent him by his rustic neighbors, in the shape of a muskmelon, which reached him safely, and, being uncommonly fine, afforded a luxurious repast to him and his military suite. He used to write frequently, nay, constantly, to his family, giving the account of Burgoyne's movements, which information was communicated as regularly to the people in the neighborhood. He assured my father he should have the earliest information of every thing important, and requested him to remain at home as long as possible, for the sake of setting an example of confidence to his neighbors. He did not know, however, how few were left to follow such an example. Almost every body who could do so, moved off, and these were the first to invent and propagate slanders against St. Clair and Schuyler.

It is a fact, that a story circulated at this time, which had some influence upon the discontented and ignorant, that these two generals had been bought up by Burgoyne, who had actually fired silver balls into their camp, and that in a few days more they would join the enemy. Our personal danger was first realized by us, in the following manner.

CHAPTER XIII.

FOR some days no information was received from our troops, who were supposed to be entrenched at Mosses creek for the purpose of making a stand. We had no idea that they were so dispirited by their retreat as we afterwards found them to be, and not being apprised of the exact state of affairs, we were wrapped in fond security until our danger was suddenly brought home to us by one of the startling incidents attendant upon an enemy's approach. It was in August, and we had just risen from dinner, rendered doubly grateful from an appetite gained in "the field at harvest home." My father had remained in the neighborhood of the invaders' army much longer than most of his friends, and relying upon the advantages of early advice from our army, pursued his agricultural avocations with his usual diligence. It was then, as I have before mentioned, that we were just risen from the dinner table, when one of my uncle's negroes came running to the house with eyes dilated in direct proportion to the danger, or, perhaps, more mathematically, as the square of the distance. It was some time

before our Mercury could recover sufficient breath
to confirm the horrors that played in his eyes.
After waiting for a few moments for the return of
his natural functions, we learned from him that an
Indian had been discovered in the orchard near the
house, evidently intending to shoot a person belonging to the family, who was at work in the garden;
the blacks, however, had given the alarm, and the
man escaped into the house, while at the same
moment six other savages rose from their place
of concealment and ran into the woods. This was
on our side of the river. The savages that remained
with Burgoyne were continually for miles in advance of him, on his flanks, reconnoitering our
movements and beating up the settlements. Their
cruelty was not to be restrained, and after the death
of Miss McCrea, whom I have often seen, they
were not at all checked by the animadversions and
threats of Sir John himself. My father, on learning the fact of their approach, went immediately
over to his brother's house, which was about one
fourth of a mile off, to ascertain what was to be
done for the safety of the families. He found him
making every exertion to move away, and the
domestics busily engaged in getting every thing
ready. During my father's absence my mother,
who was a resolute woman, one fitted for the times

in which she lived, was industriously placing the
most valuable of her clothing in a cask; and at her
instance I went out with some of our servants to
catch a pair of fleet horses and harness them as fast
as possible to the wagon. To those who now sit
quietly in their own shady bowers, or by the fire-
side long endeared by tranquility and happiness, I
leave it to be imagined with what feelings we
hastened to abandon our home and fly for safety, we
knew not whither. The men of this generation
can never know what were the sorrows of those
fathers that saw their children exposed to dangers
and to death, and what the agonies of those mothers
who pressed their offspring to their bosom, in the
constant apprehension of seeing them torn from
their embraces to become the victims of savage
cruelty.

I can never forget, and I feel it now impossible,
with sufficient force to describe, the distress of our
family at this moment of peril and alarm. The
wagon was soon at the door, and as my father came
up he directed us to carry a few loads down to the
river, and place them in a light batteau which belonged to us, and was fastened to the shore at the
meadow's bank near the ferry. The first time I
went down alone and soon unloaded the contents
of the wagon. The distance I had to go was about

a quarter of a mile. The road ran down the meadow, and was cut through the bank on the river side, in order to make it easy of ascent. Between the upland and lowland of our farm there was a board fence, and a few bars were usually placed across the road. The second time having some heavier articles to carry, I was accompanied by my father. As we approached the fence, which he had left down, we saw the third bar across the road so as effectually to prevent our passing through. What does this mean, exclaimed he. I was breathless with agitation, and stopped the horses. My father sprang out, making an expressive motion with his hand to keep back for a few moments. Warily and carefully turning his eye in every direction, he approached the bar, and let it down. I drove on, he jumped in, and we lost no time in hastening home. The circumstance gave us great uneasiness. When we reached home he made minute inquiries among his laborers and blacks if any of them had been down to the meadow. He found that none of them had been away from the house. He then formed the conclusion that some Indians had passed along that way, and supposing we had crossed the river, and got beyond their reach (for we were hid from their observation by being under the bank at the river side), had gone away. The danger was so near as to induce him to make more speed and use greater precaution. A gun was loaded and placed in my hands and I patrolled about the house with a feeling of some responsibility. I strained my eye to detect the least appearance of motion, presented my piece at every waving bush, but was not under the necessity of discharging it. A friendly neighbor, who was also anxious to ascertain the state of things, came up at this time, and assisted me in keeping guard — my father, in the interim, placed the family in the wagon — among other precautions, he had opened his pens and let loose upon the world six noble porkers, whom he had assiduously been feeding, determined that the enemy should, at least, have the trouble of catching before they should cook them — he also buried, in the road, some valuable domestic utensils, which we recovered, some years afterwards, in perfect preservation. At last we bade adieu to our homestead, and arrived safely at the river. At about 5 o'clock P. M. my father crossed over with the family at the ferry, while I and one of the blacks were put into a small canoe, and we proceeded down the stream as fast as we could ply our paddles. We joined the family at Vandenbergh's, eight miles down the river, where we obtained further information — we learned that a party of Indians had been going from our neighborhood to the south-east, after surprising a farmer by the name of Lake.   While working at his trade as a carpenter, in an out-house near his dwelling, he was surprised by the salution from the savages of *sago*.   With great presence of mind he said *sago*, in reply to them.   He saw that resistance would be vain, and therefore continued quietly at work; they looked at him a few moments, and then went towards his house, but took nothing from it. On coming out they discovered an oven which gave signs of having just been heated; they opened it, and finding it full of bread, took each of them a loaf.   In a field adjacent a sheep came straying near them; one of them instantly shot it, and in a few moments it was cut into quarters and carried off. Lake was a resolute man, and observed, if he could only have had any chance with them he never would have suffered them all to escape alive.   At Vandenbergh's we found my father, who had arrived there first, and was keeping an anxious lookout for us on the shore.

CHAPTER XIV.

W<small>E</small> found, on landing, a number of people, who, like ourselves, had been driven from their homes. I scarcely ever witnessed a greater scene of hurry and confusion than was now presented to our view. I had been amused by the novelty and pleased with the variety of incidents which attended our own flight, but the distress of the groups around us changed the current of my feelings, and excited my deepest sympathy. We passed the night amongst them. Some of them obtained accommodations within doors; some were happy to be under the cover of the cattle sheds, while others stretched themselves in their wagons, and endeavored to snatch a few moments of repose. Early in the morning the sleepers were awakened, and no fresh rumors alarmed them to any very hasty movements. Indeed, my father rather rashly resolvd to return home, accompanied by a few congenial spirits, to get further information of the enemy, and, if possible, to save some of his cattle and farming stock— I say rashly, as Burgoyne was expected down with his army every hour. Soon after he was gone the

L^T GEN. BURGOYNE.

whole body of the people at Vandenbergh's moved
off towards Stillwater; a general panic now prevailing among them, which seemed every hour to
increase. My father, however, safely reached his
house, and succeeded in getting off part of his stock.
He immediately pushed for the Hoosick river, whch
he intended to cross, and then pass over into New
England. Corresponding arrangements had been
made on our part, when he left us, to rejoin him
there. Our procession of flying inhabitants wore
a strange and melancholy appearance. A long
cavalcade of wagons, filled with all kinds of furniture, not often selected by the owners with reference
to their use or value on occasions of alarm, stretched
along the road, while others on horseback, and
here and there two mounted at once upon a steed
panting under the double load, were followed by a
crowd of pedestrians, *sed longo intervallo*. These
found great difficulty in keeping up with the
rapid flight of their mounted friends. Here and
there would be seen some humane person assisting
the more unfortunate, by relieving them of the
packs and bundles with which they were incum-
bered; but, generally, a principle of selfishness
prevented much interchange of friendly offices.
Every one for himself was the constant cry. After
my father's departure he committed to me the care

10

of his wagon and horses, and the safe conduct of
my mother and the family. Unfortunately for me,
when we left home, I had selected the most valuable and spirited horses, and so restive did I now find
them that they completely overcame my strength
and wearied my patience. They were continually
attempting to run past the wagons ahead of me,
and were every instant making an effort to get off
the road. My chafed and blistered hands could no
longer restrain them. I saw that in a few moments
more I should be unable to prevent the lamentable
consequences. My mother was then nursing a
young infant which she now held in her arms, and
felt an indescribable anxiety on that account. She
succeeded in making a person, who came along side
of us, sensible of our distress, and hired him to
drive the horses at the then dear rate of a shilling
a mile, but he soon gave up from inability to control them, having far less skill than myself. In this
dilemma, with tears in her eyes, and despair in her
looks, she got out of the wagon, and picking up a
stout club in the road, walked on for many miles
at the head of the unruly animals, and with her
infant on one arm, actually kept them back and
restrained them from breaking the line by striking them over the heads with the stick she held in
the other. And so great was each individual's

anxiety for himself, that not a person in the throng
offered to assist her.   I knew of but one other mother who, in our part of the country, endured
greater hardships than mine.   And I shall, doubtless, be understood, when I refer my readers to the
fair and intelligent heroine of Tomhannock, who
has left behind her an account of her flight from
home, about the same time, with a young child she
dearly loved, unprotected, friendless, and exposed
to danger at every step of a most perilous journey.
When we reached Stillwater it was evident that
our retreat was well timed, for the advance guard
of Gen. Schuyler's army arrived almost as soon as
we did.   They encamped there, and the increasing
confusion and noise, every moment, added new difficulties to those we already were doomed to encounter.   We remained here all night, as it was our
intention next day to cross the river and overtake
my father, who, by this time, we supposed several
miles on his way to Massachusetts.   Some of his
brothers also agreed to take the same direction, and
early in the morning we crossed the river and
traveled a whole day through a penetrating rain
and over the worst of roads.   We had gone about
fifteen miles when darkness overtook us, and we
were far from any place of shelter.   We had no
alternative but to remain there till morning, and

selecting the driest place in the marsh where we were fairly stuck fast, some beds were taken out of the wagons and laid on the ground. On these my mother reposed, if the wakeful and comfortless hours could be said to have been repose. We were afraid to light any fire, for we knew the woods were filled with tories and Indians. To our hard fate necessity, therefore, compelled us to submit. Cold, wet and dreary was the night, yet it was not without its consolation, for before morning broke upon our wretched bivouac my father arrived, to our great astonishment and pleasure. He had sent off his cattle to the eastward — and then he returned to Stillwater — finding us gone, he followed our track, and at length overtook us at this spot. We started as soon as it was light enough to travel, and that day reached San Coick, in the south part of Cambridge, where we were received by some distant connexions with much hospitality.

CHAPTER XV.

W E afterwards learned that at a place called Tull's
Mills, upon the very route we had taken, a man had
been killed only two hours after we had passed.
We were now resting ourselves at San Coick; but
as the bird which lights upon the waving branch,
rather than in the denser foliage of the trees, that
it may more easily wing its flight, so we hovered
upon the borders of the army, that we might again
disengage ourselves upon the approach of the enemy,
and escape to some other place of security. The
second day after our arrival my father went back to
Stillwater to secure or bring away another wagon
and pair of horses. The whole army were now there,
unable to maintain themselves in their former position, and indeed being on the retreat. On his return he was startled at hearing a heavy discharge of
musketry. He fancied, as many others did, that a
general engagement had commenced, but it proved
to be only a preparation for cleaning muskets that
had grown foul and almost useless during the rainy
weather, and for which General Schuyler with his
usual prudence saw a favorable opportunity.

The noise was distinctly heard for many miles. As my father approached within a few miles of San Coick, a person who was riding with him in his wagon, and whose fears gave a telescopic accuracy to his vision, discovered at the foot of the hill they were descending, a party of men crossing the road at about one hundred and fifty yards distance before them. They were moving off to the north with great rapidity in single file, and were at least forty in number. It was about dusk when this unpleasant vision occured. It was doubtful whether they were on the retreat or proceeding to set an ambush for the two travelers.

My father took counsel of his courage, and with a dash of resolution, peculiar to himself, determined to make the most of his perilous situation. He gave the whip to his horses, put them to their full speed, while at the same time he and his companion shouted as loud and as fast as possible: Hurrah! come on men, here, here, hurrah!! making the woods reëcho to their cries. What precise effect this stratagem had could never be ascertained, for certain it is the forty were no more seen, and the travelers reached their place of destination in safety.

A circumstance took place at this time within my knowledge which caused much conversation among those of us acquainted with the facts.   There was a schoolmaster by the name of Frazer, who had been employed by our neighbors to teach their children, and by my father and uncles in particular.   He used to say he was a nephew of Capt. Frazer, who, I believe, had charge of Burgoyne's Indians, and had been his secretary, or perhaps his servant at Quebec.   He was a pensioner of the British government in consequence of a wound he had received in its service.   About the time that Burgoyne was drawing so near us this man proposed to me to go to the enemy, stating that when he reached them he could get 1,800*l* which was due him from the crown. I presume he wanted me as a witness to prove that he had never taken up arms against his country. I declined going ; but he succeeded in enticing the very person who was with my father during the scene above mentioned.   These deserters had not proceeded far, however, from San Coick, before both the knight errant and his squire were taken prisoners by an American patrol, and under circumstances showing their intentions too plainly to be misunderstood.   My father was astonished at Frazer, but nevertheless offered to become security for his good behavior.   At first it was refused, but after some trouble they consented, and Frazer was relieved from the threatened horrors of confinement, and became a sort of hanger-on of our family until better times. We soon discovered that our proposed retreat into New England would not do, for provisions were scarce and fodder for cattle was not to be had there. We then turned our faces towards Albany, and our friends at San Coick came along with us. The restive horses were now driven by another hand, and I rode on horseback in the character of a drover, or cattle driver. We went through Tomhannock to Lansingburgh, where another adventure occurred of a similar nature.

CHAPTER XVI.

As we went through the settlement of Lansingburgh some of the cows of my uncle's drove had
strayed away from the main body, and, leaving the
road, had entered some of the adjacent fields,
tempted, no doubt, by the appearance of something eatable in that quarter. A few of us entered
a ravine in hopes of finding them there. Hallooing
like drovers we soon got them out of the gully,
and came out at the lower part of the town towards
Mr. Lansing's. Here we all huddled under a large
barn to escape a heavy shower, and were scarcely
ensconced when an old man came tottering up to us
with his face covered with mud, and his clothes
stripped from his back; a more distressed object
could scarcely be imagined. My father, however,
recognized him as Squire ——, who informed him
that he was just liberated in the condition we saw
him, by a party of tories and Indians, upwards of
200 in number, by whom he had been taken prisoner. He informed us that he was with them in
the very gully through which we passed in search
of the cattle. Said he, " You had a narrow escape,

11

but they were too busy in examining me as to the number of our troops, the places of rendezvous, and state of public feeling." They were therefore silent as we passed. They had robbed the old man of a beaver hat, his silver shoe buckles and most of his clothes, and then sent him away. This was all done in broad daylight. We could scarcely credit his story, but his respectability and actual appearance left us no room to doubt. Burgoyne always moved with great precaution — was always seeking intelligence; and if ever a general was well served by his scouts, or an invading army assisted by disaffected inhabitants, his was. Rank toryism and "infamous venality" fought against us on his side, and I am persuaded our cause was sustained by the Lord of battles, or we should have sunk under the difficulties which beset us. It is well known that the ancestors of some of the most respectable families now in the city of Albany were actually confined or sent out of the state in consequence of their secret exertions in favor of Burgoyne. From Lansingburgh we hastened to Troy, and while at the ferry waiting our turn for crossing the report of a rifle was heard just back of us in the hollow now filled with thriving factories. We soon learned that a man had been shot and scalped by the Indians, who were lurking in the vicinity. My mother was

alarmed, and though accustomed to hair-breadth
escapes, desired to incur no more of them. She
urged my father to cross as soon as possible, which
he did. It was dark, however, before we made
good our passage. We drove our wagons and stock
into a barn, where we were happy to be sheltered
from a heavy rain. We were not there long before
a detachment of troops on their way to join the
camp came up and entered the barn pell mell. We,
who had escaped from our enemies, had now as
much as we could do to protect ourselves from our
friends. They went about in the dark feeling in
the wagons, and taking every thing they could lay
their hands on. The doctrine of *meum* and *tuum*
was not recognized by the marauders, and we were
obliged to stretch ourselves at full length over our
goods in order to frustrate their attempts at pilfer-
ing. The night was passed in this way, and it
was only in the morning when they went off that
we were enabled to get a little sleep. We then
came on to Albany. The roads were filled with
people flying like ourselves, who feared all was
lost; a general despondency prevailed. As we came
near the residence of the Patroon, as the head of
the Rensselaer family is still termed, we were invited by some person of his establishment to remain
and recruit ourselves at the old brick house now

occupied as his office, on the right hand side of the road, shaded with venerable trees.   For a fortnight we remained there, being allowed a room for our family.   We were here treated in the kindest manner; our stock was permitted to graze in the adjacent fields.   I should do injustice to the feelings of our grateful hearts if I did not take the opportunity of expressing a sense of our obligations for this kindness, although fifty years have elapsed since we received their attentions.   It gives me pleasure to think that amidst the vicissitudes which have overtaken other distinguished families of that day, this has not only sustained its character for virtue, benevolence and philanthropy, but for well deserved wealth.   While it makes no claim on the public for ostentatious actions, it silently performs its duty to society in such a manner as to win the respect and regard of all.   The present proprietor of the immense estate of that family is universally beloved, and wears the palm decreed to modest and unassuming merit, to benevolent and patriotic worth.   If this should ever come under his eye, let not the honest compliment of an old friend cause him a single blush.   The world decrees him the celebrity due his amiable character, and the concurrence of individual opinion is but a leaf in his chaplet.[1]

---

[1] The late Stephen Van Rensselaer.

Having recruited ourselves after our fatigue and anxiety we proceeded to Bethlehem, and were there kindly received by our relations.   This I think proper to mention, for I may state that as distrust and selfishness often characterized the times which I am describing, many, in referring back to that period, can remember but too well the coolness which was shown to them by persons in whose friendship they expected to find sympathy and relief.   Too many in looking back to those days of peril and alarm find cause to regret the suspicion which seemed to color every transaction.   It was a critical period, and every one seemed to imagine his own danger and difficulty as great as it was possible to encounter; and under this impression ties the most natural and affecting were like ropes of sand, broken at the very touch.

CHAPTER XVII.

FROM Bethlehem we made a visit to another relative of my father's, from whom we also received much kindness and some assistance. Here the family remained until they returned home. About the time that the hostile armies at the north began to approach each other, and our forces left their encampment at Van Schaick's island, which still remains in possession of the descendants of the then owners, and moved back again to Stillwater, towards the enemy, my father had a great curiosity to be present at some of the expected battles. After the British had destroyed all the crops about Gen. Schuyler's farm, and reduced a beautiful spot to a scene of distress and poverty, they moved on to a place called Dovacote, before they crossed the river, opposite to which one spot was rendered interesting by an accident of a singular kind. I have often stood upon the very place where Major Ackland's tent took fire, and where Lady Harriet and himself were nearly lost in the flames. As this is a reminiscence not generally known, I will state what I believe the fact was. The Major being with the advance guard, and obliged to be very diligent in attending to his command, in consequence of the difficulty and danger of his position, kept a candle burning in his tent. A Newfoundland dog, of which they were very fond, unfortunately pushed the candle from a table or a chair, where it was standing. It fell against the side of the tent, and instantly the whole was in a blaze; a soldier who was keeping guard near them rushed in and dragged Major Ackland from the flames, while Lady Harriet crept out almost unconsciously through the back part of the tent. When she looked round she saw with horror her husband rushing into the flames in search of her. Again the soldier brought him out, though not without considerable injury to both. Every thing in the tent was consumed; but the lovers were too happy to see each other in safety to regret the loss of their camp equipage. It may not be amiss to state, that this admired and beautiful woman had already been subjected to great inconvenience and distress before the army arrived at Saratoga. She had been distinguished by her devotion and unremitting attention to her husband, when he lay sick at Chamblee in a miserable hut, encountering every inconvenience and subjected to every privation. She was indeed not only the idol of her husband, but the admiration of the army, continually making little presents to the officers belonging to her husband's corps, whenever she had any thing among her stores worthy of acceptance. She experienced in return from them every attention which could mitigate the hardships she daily was obliged to encounter.

When her husband was wounded at Hubbardton, she again, like a guardian angel, hovered round him and watched him until restored to health. The moment she heard of his being wounded she hastened from Montreal, where she had intended to remain, and crossed the lake in opposition to her husband's injunctions, resolved to share his fate and be separated from him no more.

My father's first visit to the camp was on the evening of the day of battle, which occurred on the 7th October. The troops were very much elated with their success, although having so decided a superiority in numbers. It was a current saying among the men, that the battle had been brought on by the enemy's attempting a forage, and that Wilkinson, then a major, informed Gen. Gates they offered him battle. His reply was, "Send the old wagoner to see." This name, given to Col. Morgan, was a cant phrase in the army. Gen. Gates, relying on Morgan's great intrepidity and good sense, kept him usually in advance. It was eleven o'clock at night before all our troops got back to the camp. Such noise and

confusion were new to my father. He often
mentioned the impressions he received upon this
occasion. The noise of drums, the cries of the
wounded, the hailing of sentinels, the moving
lights, the groups of soldiers all eager for another
contest, gave animation and spirit to the scene.
Among the losses of the enemy was Sir Francis
Clarke, aid to Burgoyne, a young man of brilliant
talents, mortally wounded and a prisoner. Major
Ackland was wounded and again separated from
the woman he loved, who during the action had
remained within reach of our cannon, listening to
every sound with heart breaking emotions.

CHAPTER XIX.

IT was on the 8th of October, if I am not mistaken, that Burgoyne's retreat was first discovered. The news created an intoxication of joy in the American camp. My father being well mounted, and anxious to see every thing that could be seen, and also having a thorough knowledge of the country roads, proposed to two friends, Mr. Swart and Mr. Schuyler, to go forward for the purpose of obtaining intelligence. They started, taking a private road which came out at Saratoga opposite the church, and there, at a short distance from them, actually saw the British troops passing by. In consequence of their excessive fatigue, and a tremendous rain and thunder storm, they were all day getting there. My father always claimed the credit with his companions, of having saved the old church from being burned. A soldier was seen approaching it with fire, when they immediately shouted to the man with all their might. He dropped the brand and ran off—they in the same instant turned their horses into the woods, and made off at full speed. My father, although he arrived late that afternoon in the camp, obtained a fresh horse, and reached Albany at 11 o'clock that night, bringing the joyful news of Burgoyne's retreat.

I ought not to forget that Lady Harriet Ackland was written to by her husband after his capture, and Major Wilkinson attempted with a flag to carry the letter to the enemy's camp. He was repulsed at every quarter. When the enemy retreated to Saratoga she asked permission of General Burgoyne to go to her husband, leaving it, however, at his option to decide against her application, if he thought it would be contrary to propriety under existing circumstances. It is represented that the British commander was thunderstruck at the application, but gave her leave to proceed, although he was utterly unable to afford any assistance. After her fatigue, and after being drenched in a heavy rain of twelve hours, she instantly proceeded on. The celebrated letter of Gen. Burgoyne to Gen. Gates on the occasion has often been admired as a specimen of that talent for composition which afterwards distinguished the author of the *Narrative*, and several elegant comedies well known to the literary public.

From the wife of a soldier she obtained a little spirit and water, and with this to sustain her she set out in an open boat, accompanied by the British chaplain Brudenell, her own waiting maid, Sarah Pollard, and her husband's valet de chambre, who had been severely wounded in searching through the field of battle for his master when he was first missing.

An impression has gone abroad, sanctioned not only by gentlemen belonging to Burgoyne's army, but by that general himself, that this ill fated and amiable female was kept all night in the boat, and not permitted to land until morning. This is not the fact. In ten minutes after the boat was hailed by the sentinel of the advance guard she was invited to the quarters of Major Dearborn (afterward so distinguished as a general officer), where she received every attention in his power to bestow, and was made happy by the intelligence of her husband's safety. In the morning before sunrise she was on her way down the river to Albany, under the guidance and protection of some of our friends. The resolution and firmness of this lady excited a great sensation throughout our camp, while the tender devotion which she displayed towards her husband, "won her golden opinions of all sorts of people."

The maid who attended her has very lately died, and her devotion to her mistress was made the subject of an engraving which was published in 1784.

Lady Harriet joined her husband at Albany, and remained with him till he was enabled to be removed to the city of New York, whence he sailed for England.

The sequel of her story is worth remembering. Major Ackland, soon after his return to England, became involved in a quarrel at a dinner table, from the circumstance of his defending the bravery of the Americans.

A duel ensued, and the major was killed at the first fire. Lady Harriet for a time lost her senses through grief, but after a time accepted the hand of the reverend chaplain whose fate had so strongly been linked with hers in descending the Hudson together.[1]

I have in vain attempted to trace the subsequent history of this admirable woman.

---

[1] An error, see note in appendix.

CHAPTER XX.

A CIRCUMSTANCE took place about this time which made considerable noise amongst our friends. It was the death of Major Van V., a very brave man, who was killed by the enemy in an attempt to visit his farm at Schaghticoke. His family had been sent to Albany at an early day; but when Burgoyne was on the retreat he could not repress his desire to visit his former home. Unfortunately he took no guard with him, and was accompanied by but one person, who was a neighbor. They both carried rifles. After crossing the river at Yates's they took a road that wound up round a field to the fort, which was on the rising ground beyond. Scarcely had they reached the turn of the road before a volley was poured in on them from the right: Major Van V. instantly fell, but recovering himself rose on his knees, and he and his companion fired together. They loaded as rapidly as possible, but before they were ready to fire a second time another volley was poured in upon them by their assailants. The major then fired and fell, crying out to his companion, "I am a dead man, save yourself if you can!" His companion leaped the fence, passed through a cornfield, and taking a marsh, leaped forward from bog to bog in order to leave no track behind by which he could be pursued. In this way he reached the river side, and ran up the banks under cover of the rocks to the upper end of Van Antwerp's reefs, through which he waded to the island in the river at that place, and thence crossed to the west side. He reached the American camp unhurt. A party was sent from thence to bring Major Van V. in; they found him at the place described, hacked to pieces and scalped. But they also found three Indians dead in the adjacent field; an extraordinary circumstance, which showed that the major and his companion behaved with courage and coolness, notwithstanding their surprise and the disparity of force. His body was brought to Albany and buried; but his unfortunate wife was not permitted to see the corpse, it was so sadly mutilated by his savage enemies.

I mentioned that my father had arrived with the news of the retreat. The intelligence was joyful to us. He ordered the black to get three horses ready early in the morning to take us back to Saratoga. Our sleep, though not sound, was filled with pleasant dreams. Early as the day dawned all were on the move but my mother, who remained behind. We met on the road great numbers of wounded men belonging to both armies. A great many were carried on litters, which were blankets fastened to a frame of four poles. I never saw the effects of war until now. In camp there was something of "pomp and circumstance," which rather animated than depressed the spirits. But the sight of these wretched people, pale and lifeless, with countenances of an expression peculiar to gunshot wounds, as the surgeons have truly informed us, and the sound of groaning voices, as each motion of the litter renewed the anguish of their wounds, filled me with horror and sickness of heart. And is public happiness then bought at the price of individual wretchedness? Must blood and tears and sorrow be the result of even the most just and righteous controversies? The human heart, "a tangled yarn," brings a curse on its own plans. Even its virtues are allied to the demons of its fallen nature, and will never be separated until humanity shall wear a brighter form in days of millenial glory. We were much affected with what we saw on our short journey; and the remembrance cannot be effaced.

We reached the American camp and drove through it to the bank of the river opposite my uncle's farm. We got out and walked along the bank to see if there was any thing to aid us in getting across. My father luckily recognized a Capt. Knute, of the bateau men, who kindly offered us the use of a scow, and, indeed, saw us safely over the river. We drove that night to our own home. But oh, how much changed! It looked like a military post, to which use it was actually converted. A thousand eastern militia were quartered around the premises. We began to think we had not gained much by coming on at this juncture. My father, however, entered the house in the dark, and, being familiar with the passages and rooms, made his way into the stove room, which he naturally thought would be most comfortable. Having brought a candle from the wagon with him, he deliberately lighted it at the stove. The moment it glimmered a person jumped off his bed, and observed to my father with as much twang as was agreeable, " You seem to be considerable acquainted here." My father's reply was, " I used to be." The stranger rejoined, " You are the owner may be." My father answered " No! I find some here before me." " O, well," continued the speaker, " you shall be *accommodated*." At this instant the steady blaze of the candle showed the room to be occupied by a number of persons, and there appeared no probability of our receiving the promised accommodation. But he spoke as one having

13

authority, when he exclaimed. "Stir boys, stir; clear the way, here is the owner come!" They yawned and grunted, and got out of the way with unexpected good nature. He also placed a guard over our wagon to protect it from *invasion*. My father, in order to return his civilities, brought in some spirits to the officer, and a social glass was handed round. It was an unexpected happiness to the kind hearted Yankee. The draught was repeated until sleep came to refresh us after our fatigues. Stretched on pallets of straw, we laid ourselves down; and after strange vicissitudes of hope and fear we sunk to rest once more in our own house, every ill and every fatigue forgotten.

CHAPTER XXI.

THE next day brought its variety; we discovered that our fellow lodgers were troops from Sheffield, Mass., and, if I remember right, were some of those militiamen who refused to stay with the army until Burgoyne should be compelled to surrender. Next morning I accompanied my father to the camp, where all was excitement and animation. It is a fact, that the troops did not eat in the ardor of pursuit with that appetite which is the soldier's characteristic. The demands of nature were forgotten. A floating bridge was constructed during this day over the river opposite Gen. Gates's quarters. It was made of boards, and was a kind of raft secured by cables and ropes on both shores. Over this floating structure a brisk foraging was kept, and it was our fate to lose something more in consequence. When we had deserted our home we left our crops standing in the field. During our absence they had been kindly cut and piled in shocks, as we termed them, by the English and Tories. A bridge of boats had been constructed by Burgoyne's army, for the convenience of foraging, in the same way as was now done by our troops. Our wheat having thus been prepared for use, circumstances alone prevented them from completing their harvest. Our commissaries found it all ready at their hands. Bundle after bundle was pitched into the wagons, and it was carried over to the camp for the use of the horses as it was fit for nothing else. The wheat was taken without a word being said. My father waived his own rights entirely, but when he saw the wagons returning to the farm after the wheat was gone, he suspected his rye was about to share a similar fate. A wry face was very natural. He immediately crossed over to the farm, and by going through the fields, he succeeded in getting ahead of the wagons just as they were about to enter the enclosures; at this instant he seized a long stake from the fence, and took post near the bars, where the wagons must necessarily pass. The commissary, a continental officer, and in full dress, ordered the driver in front to take down the bars. My father said he should resist the effort at the risk of his life. The wagoner had no wish to attempt the passage. The commissary dismounted, drew his sword, and approached the spot as if he at least was not to be intimidated. The stake was raised in a most unequivocal manner. One instant more and the officer's brains, if he had any, were in danger of a concussion. "Touch those bars at your peril." The officer called the wagoners to his assistance. They declined interfering, stating that they did not wish to get themselves into difficulty. The officer behaved with discretion. He did not touch the fence, but remounting his steed, drove off the ground, followed by a train of empty wagons. When they were fairly gone, my father again headed them, and crossing the bridge, which was constantly crowded with persons, he arrived in camp and stationed himself near the head quarters, waiting the result. The commissary, as he anticipated, instantly went to Gen. Gates, taking his empty wagons with him. The general asked him the reason why he returned empty. The officer replied that the owner forcibly resisted him. "Did you attempt to take lawfully? Did you take appraisers with you?" "No sir," drawled out the subaltern. "You blockhead," said the general, with more warmth than regard to etiquette, "he would have been justified had he resisted you to the last extremity." While this was going on some one hinted that my father was the owner, and he was recognized by the general. "We must have the grain for our horses," said he. His manner was, however, mild and conciliating. My father instantly replied, "My necessities are greater than yours, general. You have taken all my wheat: it is hard that my last grain should be taken from me." General Gates seemed touched with the reply, but added, "My dear sir, I respect this necessity as much as you do, but it is easier for an individual to provide for his wants, than me to manage for a whole army. This is the crisis of our fate. The salvation of this country rests on the issue of events now taking place, and in the result you and all of us are deeply interested." My father "thought like a sage, though he felt as a man." "Then take it, sir, but let it be done in the manner prescribed by law; my country demands the sacrifice, and cheerfully will I make it."

Appraisers were then appointed on the spot, and they proceeded together and asssessed the loss sustained by us. A nominal advantage it proved to be in the end, for after taking every thing, my father never even got a certificate of the quantity carried away, nor any voucher whatever from the commissaries. The quantity taken was so considerable as to induce my father afterwards to go to Poughkeepsie to obtain some recognition of this sacrifice, supported by the necessary papers to establish the fact; the quartermaster general declined doing any thing in relation to it. This is one of the thousand instances of the petty tyranny and injustice of public agents in the days of the revolution, and is given to corroborate the facts set forth in our most authentic histories. My father died a creditor to the government in more than this one instance. His posterity have never gained any thing by his devotion to the cause.

CHAPTER XXII.

W E remained busily at work on our farm, surrounded by all the circumstance of war. The enemy at length, overcome by the difficulties of an untenable position, had retreated to Fish kil, and crossing the creek, took possession of the heights beyond, with an intention of retreating to Fort Edward. I made an excursion with a neighbor, up the west side of the river to see what was going on. At one place I was witness to the military achievements of militia that lay concealed along the bank, and waylaid every thing that promised them any plunder. Burgoyne's bateaux and scows during these his retrograde movements were busily engaged in moving up with his baggage and provisions as well as they were able. The militia took possession of all they could lay their hands on, but were at length menaced by the general order of the 12th September, with the utmost severity of the law, "for the many mean and scandalous transactions of persons who seek more after plunder than the honor of doing their duty in a becoming soldierlike manner." Nay, the officers themselves were alluded to

in the same order. "Officers who know their duty
and have virtue to practice it, will not be seeking
plunder when they ought to be doing their best
service in the field."

As I have intended to give a faithful description of
the scenes which were witnessed by us all, I hope
I shall not be considered as having "aught set down
in malice."

A few bateaux and scows were passing along as
I arrived — they were loaded with military stores,
the baggage of the officers, and the women who
followed their "soger laddies." A few well directed
shots brought them to the bank. A rush took
place for the prey. Every thing was hauled out
and carried back into a low swampy place in the
rear, and a guard placed over it. What was not
convertible to money or necessary for use was
burned, and when the plunder was divided among
the captors, the poor females, trembling with fear,
were released and permitted to go off in a boat to
the British army, a short distance above, on the
other side of the river. Such a collection of tanned
and leathern visages was never before seen. Poorly
clad, their garments bearing the marks of hardships, and their persons war-worn and weary, the
women were objects of my sincere pity. The wife
and bairns of the soldier have often excited the sym-

14

pathy of the poet, and have been pointed in the
sweetest language of the muse to their only consolation.

> "When the vengeful strife is over,
> Then ye'll meet nae mair to sever,
> Till the day ye die, lassie."

But I believe even the less sentimental and
desponding followers of the camp, though not elevated to any rank in the imaginations of the bards,
are deserving subjects of pity, if not of poetry. I
could not help looking at these women without
involuntarily thinking of their long distance from
their native villages in England and in Germany,
the dangers they had passed, and all the hardships
they must have encountered, not forgetting their
exposure a few moments before to the fire of our
eager marksmen, and the random shots that might
have terminated their miserable existence. Indeed,
while we were all together on the bank, some contest of a similar kind had created a sharp firing
across the river near us, and the shot came rattling
over our heads in the trees and bushes like rain pat-
tering on the pavement.

Near the marsh my companion and I had occasion to assist one of the very kind of persons probably alluded to in the general order of Gen. Gates.

As we approached a small creek we saw a horse

and his rider lying floundering in the mud, in apparent inextricable confusion. On coming up we ascertained that his immobility was partly owing to his having a bag about his person full of musket balls, which he had picked up he said, in a shallow place in the river, and which now hung like a mill-stone round his neck. We, however, assisted him to quit the slough, and remount his steed with the bag of bullets, and he slowly trotted away.

CHAPTER XXIII.

EVERY moment the scene was growing more interesting. As we came near the main body of the enemy, which we approached within three fourths of a mile, and while we were looking round to observe the movements of different detachments about us, which we could do very distinctly, we observed a flash from a cannon, and almost instantly saw a ball come out of the Saratoga church, apparently deadened by the resistance it had met. It passed over our heads with a slight whizzing, and struck in the bank behind us, at the distance of three hundred yards. In a few moments another, its fellow, passed through the church in the same manner, and struck in the same bank beyond us. I judged that the range of these shots was about a mile. The church long exhibited the marks of the balls; but it was pulled down some years ago, and another of more modern appearance is now devoted in its place to religious worship. We did not remain in our position any longer. We were well satisfied that we had exposed ourselves sufficiently for the present to gratify our curiosity. An anecdote recurs to my recollection which shows the daring of our soldiers. It is well known that the east side of the river was lined with militia. One of them discovered a number of the enemy's horses feeding in a meadow of Gen. Schuyler's, opposite; he asked permission of his captain to go over and get one of them. It was given, and the man instantly stripped, and swam forward across the river. He ascended the bank, and selecting a bay horse for his victim, approached the animal, seized him, and mounted him instantly. This last was the work of a moment. He forced the horse into a gallop, plunged down the bank and brought him safely over to the American camp, although a volley of musketry was fired at him from a party posted at a distance beyond. His success was hailed with enthusiasm, and it had a corresponding effect on his own adventurous spirit. After he had rested himself he went to his officer and remarked, that it was not proper that a private should ride while his commander went on foot. So, sir, added he, if you have no objections I will go and catch another for you, and next winter when we are home, we will have our own fun in driving a pair of Burgoyne's horses. The captain seemed to think it would be rather a pleasant thing, and gave a ready consent. The fellow actually went across a second time, and with equal success brought over a horse

that matched exceedingly well with the other. The
'men enjoyed this prank very much, and it was a
circumstance familiar to almost every one in the
army at that time.

Another circumstance also occurs to me, which
happened at the same period, and shows that families were not only divided in feeling on the subject
of the war, but that the natural ties which bind the
same "kith and kin" together were not always
proof against the political animosities of the times.
When Burgoyne found that his boats were not safe,
and were in fact much nearer the main body of our
army than his own, it became necessary to land his
provisions, of which he had already been short for
many weeks, in order to prevent his being actually
starved into submission. This was done under a
heavy fire from our troops. On one of these occasions a person by the name of Mr. ———, well
known at Salem, and a foreigner by birth, and who
had at the very time a son in the British army,
crossed the river at De Ruyter's, with a person by
the name of M'Neil; they went in a canoe, and
arriving opposite to the place intended, crossed
over to the western bank, on which a redoubt called
Fort Lawrence had been placed. They crawled up
the bank with their arms in their hands, and peep-
ing over the upper edge, they saw a man in a blanket

coat loading a cart. They instantly raised their guns to fire, an action more savage than commendable. At the moment the man turned so as to be more plainly seen, when old M—— said to his companion, "Now that's my own son Hughy, but I'm dom'd for a' that if I sill not gie him a shot." He then actually fired at his own son, as the person really proved to be, but happily without effect. Having heard the noise made by their conversation and the cocking of the pieces, which the nearness of his position rendered perfectly practicable, he ran round the cart, and the ball lodged in the felly of the wheel. The report drew the attention of the neighboring guards, and the two marauders were driven from their lurking place. While retreating with all possible speed, M'Neil was wounded in the shoulder, and, if alive, carries the wound about with him to this day. Had the ball struck the old Scotchman, it is questionable whether any one would have considered it more than even handed justice commending the chalice to his own lips.

CHAPTER XXIV.

GEN. Burgoyne had been obliged to remove his goods from his bateaux to the shore, and that under a heavy fire. As the property taken from the bateaux was often left near the water, it was rumored among our people that large quantities of powder were slightly guarded, and easily accessible. My father was a keen sportsman, and he resolved to go up the river and obtain some, be the risk what it might. He started with two companions on horseback at about 11 o'clock at night, and forded the river. When they reached the shore they tied their horses together and went up the bank, near which, it was, the articles were left. The guard was stationed a short distance from them, as the fire of our troops from across the river was too heavy to permit them to remain within its range. Their position being fixed, it was not changed at night to prevent confusion in their own camp discipline. They were so near as to make it exceedingly difficult and dangerous to approach the stores. However, the three adventurers crept up the bank as silently as they could, approached some barrels which contained powder, the heads of which were loose. As they commenced the work of filling their bags they were hailed, and making no answer, were fired on by the guard. They retreated instantly down the bank, mounted their horses, and got safely off, each with about five pounds of the best British powder. It was hardly enough to have justified the attempt, but my father always prized his share of the spoil as valuable beyond price. Indeed, long after the war he retained a portion of it, and its excellent qualities were appreciated by all the Leather-stockings of our neighborhood. The adventurers reached home safely in a few hours after they started.

I will not describe what has so often been the subject of able writers, the negotiations that took place between the two commanders in relation to the surrender. The leading facts are well known. Suffice it to say, the British army was distressed beyond measure, for want of provisions and water. It was at last at the risk of life itself that a drop of it was to be had. The poor soldiers' wives alone ventured within reach of the American rifles, to snatch a few cups full from the river, which to them seemed watched by attendant furies. In the celebrated memoirs of the Baroness Riedesel she mentions that to one poor female who ventured her life in this way, to obtain water for her, some other females, and wounded officers, they expressed their gratitude by giving her twenty guineas as soon as the surrender took place, and there was a probability of her living to enjoy the donation.

While the negotiations were going on I saw Major Wilkinson go out with a flag to the enemy on the memorable occasion, when Burgoyne imprudently requested permission to ascertain whether the militia had gone off the field, a mere excuse for breaking off the treaty if he had dared. He was a fine looking young man, but plainly dressed on the occasion. As he left Gen. Gates's head quarters I happened to be present, being constantly (when I could be so) loitering about the camp. I heard the general say distinctly, "Tell Burgoyne if you are not back in an hour and a quarter I'll open every battery I have upon him." It is well known that the time elapsed, and two hours besides, which had been asked for by the British general, to take the opinion of his officers. The capitulation took place, or rather the convention, and I went home to a late dinner. The expectation of this desirable event had filled both armies with a disinclination for any further bloodshed. Any other termination of negotiations was to have been dreaded. It was hailed with universal joy, and produced the happiest consequences to our cause.

On the morning of the 17th the manner of the surrrender was adjusted. The American troops were kept within their lines, out of motives of delicacy, while the British troops left their encampment, marching out with the honors of war, and forded the creek on their way to the verge of the river where their arms were to be piled. They were obliged to march through the water for the very good reason that they had destroyed the only bridge, as well as the houses and mansion of Gen. Schuyler in the neighborhood. The light infantry waded through first, and their clean white kerseymeres were soon soiled with mud and water. They made the best of their way with their music playing a British march to the very place now occupied by the canal basin in Schuylerville. Among other things, I asked a British officer where Burgoyne was. He very politely noticed me, although I was a boy, and under circumstances that did not promise any civility from the mortified English. "He is with your general, I believe." At this time my father, near whom I was, and a Capt. Knute, approached very close to the British columns. A British officer, as they came nigh him, drew his sword, which was a very handsome one, and in the most pettish manner possible, presented it to my father, saying, "You damned rebel, take this, I have no more use for it!" Surprised at the suddenness of the movement, and scarce knowing what he did, my father kept it in his hand for an instant, and before he recovered himself the officer was gone. He felt extremely awkward with it, and much more so, as he doubted the propriety of keeping it a moment. His companion advised him to put it in some secure spot until he could place it in proper hands, or secure it as a memorial for himself and his posterity. He did, as he supposed, place it in security, but in a short time after he went to get the trophy, but it was gone, and he never heard any thing more of it.

CHAPTER XXV.

WHEN I heard that Burgoyne was at head quarters I waited no longer to observe the march of the light infantry, but ran as fast as I could to reach the marquee of Gen. Gates, now doubly interesting by the presence of the captured general. Near head quarters I met an uncle of mine, for all our family and all the neighbors round were present on this memorable occasion. I stopped a moment with him to see the light horse that were now parading for a review, preparatory to the entry of the British within the lines. They wore blue coats with white facings, their heads were covered with bear skin caps and long white hair streaming in the wind. They were, on the whole, well dressed and well mounted. My uncle bade me stop. "Remain here, there is mischief doing here, I have just heard one of the men say, that if General Schuyler shows his face here, he will put a brace of balls through him." Indeed, he was so much alarmed, not only by the threat, but by the general appearance of things in the corps, that he had resolved to go and apprise the general of the circumstances.

Although young, I gave my opinion at once, that his going would be unnecessary, for the man would not dare to fire. And so the event proved. General Schuyler and an officer with him approached them on his favorite white horse in very handsome style, and them gave the passing review, as military etiquette prescribed. He then commenced addressing the men; but what he said I did not stay to hear, as I was sensible only to the overwhelming interest attached to the person of Burgoyne. I never ascertained what was the occasion of the threat just related, but there was some dislike to General Schuyler among some of the eastern troops, that neither his character, conduct nor military services could overcome. I never can believe that he was in fault. As I approached General Gates's tent I perceived three sentinels in front; I asked them if General Burgoyne was there. They said yes, he was dining with General Gates. I then asked permission to pass within the lines. They gave me leave with the addition of a compliment for my being a little Whig. Eager beyond expression for a glimpse of the man, I stood at the side of the tent door which now and then opened as a servant passed in and out. I was soon gratified by closer observation. Near me there was an officer who was mounted and stationed a little higher up, and stood ready to receive the British troops. As they approached the lines of our camp, and were coming down the road to pass through them, our men were paraded, if I remember right, opposite the place where they were to enter, and the moment they stepped foot upon our line our drums and music struck up Yankee Doodle. At this moment the two generals came out of the marquee together. The American commander faced the road, and Burgoyne did the same, standing on his left. Not a word was said by either, and for some minutes, to the best of my recollection, they stood silently gazing on the scene before them. The one, no doubt in all the pride of honest success; the other, the victim of regret and sensibility. Burgoyne was a large and stoutly formed man, his countenance was rough and hard, and somewhat marked with scars, if I am not mistaken, but he had a handsome figure and a noble air. Gates was a smaller man with much less of manner, and destitute of that air which distinguished Burgoyne. Presently General Burgoyne, as by previous understanding, stepped back, drew his sword, and in the face of the two armies, as it were, presented it to General Gates, who received, and instantly returned it in the most courteous manner. They then returned together to the marquee. Having been fully gratified with the exhibition, I then ran up the road to which the British troops were filing off, and I saw the whole body pass before me. The light infantry, still in advance, were extraordinary men. Finer and better looking troops I never saw. They were not seen to much advantage, however, for their small-clothes and gaiters having been wet in the creek, the dust adhered more readily to them in consequence. Some of the officers were very elegant men. Captain Lord Petersham, aid to General Burgoyne, Major Kingston, adjutant general, Brigadier General Hamilton, of the English, were pointed out to me.

The Hessians came lumbering in the rear. When were they ever in advance? Indeed their equipments prevented such an anomaly. Their heavy caps were almost equal to the weight of the whole equipment of a light infantry soldier. I looked at these men with commiseration. It was well known that their services had been sold by their own petty princes, that they were collected together, if not *caught* at their churches while attending religious worship, and if we may credit the account given us, they were actually torn from their homes and handed over to the British government at so much a head, to be transported across the ocean and wage war against a people of whose history and even of whose existence they were ignorant. They were found almost totally unfit for the business they were engaged in. They were unable to march through the woods and encounter the difficulties incident to movements in our then almost unsettled country. Many of them deserted to our army before and after the convention of Saratoga. Fifty have been known to come over in one party before the surrender.

A very remarkable disease prevailed among them, if the accounts of some respectable officers attached to Burgoyne's army may be credited. While on their way down from Canada a presentiment would take possession of twenty or thirty at a time that they were going to die, and that they would never again see their fatherland. The impression could not be effaced from their minds, notwithstanding every exertion of their officers and the administering of medical remedies. A perfect *maladie du pays*, a home sickness of the most fatal kind, oppressed their spirits and destroyed their health; and a large number actually died of this disorder of the heart. This is a fact too well established to be denied, and equals anything I ever heard related of the Swiss. Among the Germans that now passed before me were the Hesse Hanau regiment, Riedesel's dragoons, and Specht's regiment, the most remarkable of the whole. The offi-

16

cers of distinction who accompanied them were Major General Riedesel, Quartermaster General Gerlach, Adjutant General Poelnitz, Secretary Langemegen, Brigadier Gen. Specht, Brigadier General Gall, and some others. The Hessians were extremely dirty in their persons, and had a collection of wild animals in their train — the only thing American they had captured. Here you saw an artilleryman leading a black grizzly bear, who every now and then would rear upon his hind legs as if he were tired of going upon all fours, or occasionally growl his disapprobation at being pulled along by his chain. In the same manner a tamed deer would be seen tripping lightly after a grenadier. Young foxes were also observed looking sagaciously at the spectators from the top of a baggage wagon, or a young racoon securely clutched under the arm of a sharp-shooter. There were a good many women accompanying the Germans, and a miserable looking set of oddly dressed, Gipsey featured females they were.

It is said that no insults were offered to the prisoners as they marched off, and they were grateful for it. However, I state it as a fact, that after they got out of the camp many of the British soldiers were extremely abusive, cursing the rebels and their own hard fate. On the other hand, at the extreme end

of the line, among the spectators and camp followers, there was some reciprocating of these
remarks with an accompaniment of tin pans.   This,
however, was not sufficiently loud to be much
remarked.   The troops were escorted by some of
our eastern militia, and crossed the river at Stillwater.

CHAPTER XXVI.

On the evening of the surrender a number of Indians and squaws, the relics of Burgoyne's aboriginal force, were brought over for safe keeping to my uncle's farm, and quartered under a strong guard in his kitchen. Without this precaution their lives would not have been safe from the exasperated militia. The murder of Miss M'Crea was but one of a number of their atrocities which hardened every heart against them, and prevented the plea of mercy from being interposed in their behalf. Among these savages were three that were between six and seven feet in height, perfect giants in form, and possessing the most ferocious countenances I ever saw. They were afterwards sent on to the northward, and discharged upon a promise not to take up arms again. With what fidelity they kept their word I never learned.

After the British army had gone detachments of our army were sent on to the south to prevent the continuation of those marauding expeditions on the Hudson, of which Esopus will long be the sad memorial. It was three days after the surrender that our camp began to be broken up. The militia were assiduous in exploring the fields for plunder and the concealed treasures of the vanquished. Immense quantities of camp furniture and fragments of every description were strewed about, and they spoiled the Egyptians.

Opposite our own house my father found a large number of hides, and a considerable quantity of tallow. This, however, neither graced his store nor greased his boots. Our friends, the *irregulars*, spared him the trouble of carrying them home. They obligingly took all off with them, out of friendship. In this way closed the evenftul history of Saratoga. Blood and carnage were succeeded by success and plunder. The clouds of battle rolled away, and discovered hundreds of earnest searchers after the relics of the tented field. My father once more commenced the labors of husbandman, and after preparing his ground in a great hurry, and sowing his winter wheat, went away to Albany to bring his wife home.

I will mention an incident that occured in relation to the memorable siege of Fort Stanwix, which shows General Schuyler's fortitude and prowess in moments of difficulty. When Colonel Willett and his companion, Lieutenant Stockwell, left the fort and got beyond the investing party, which was not done without passing through sleeping groups of savages, who lay with their arms at their side, they crossed the river, and found some horses running wild in the woods. They were soon mounted, and with the aid of their bark bridles stripped from the young trees, they made considerable progress on their journey. It is well known that they reached Saratoga and begged a reinforcement. General Schuyler called a council of his officers, and asked their advice. It is not generally known that he was opposed by them. As he walked about in the greatest anxiety urging them to come to his opinion, he overheard some of them saying "he means to weaken the army." The emotions of the veteran were always violent at the recollection of this charge, and years afterwards I have seen him shed tears as he related the incident. At the instant when he heard the remark, he found that he had bitten a pipe, which he had been smoking, into several pieces, without being conscious of what he had done. Indignantly he exclaimed, "Gentlemen, I shall take the responsibility upon myself; where is the brigadier that will take command of the relief? I shall beat up for volunteers to-morrow." The brave, the gallant, the ill-fated Arnold started up with his characteristic quickness, and offered to command the expedition. In the morning the drum beat for volunteers, and two hundred hardy fellows capable of withstanding great fatigue, offered their services and were accepted. The result of his efforts is well known, a stratagem was played off upon the Tories and Indians, which left St. Leger no alternative but a hasty retreat. To General Schuyler's promptness and fearlessness, therefore, due credit should be given.

I will here relate an anecdote in relation to this siege which I heard at the same time, and which was quite current among our people. A man by the name of Baxter, who resided in the vicinity of the fort, being a disaffected man, had been sent to Albany to be watched by the committee of safety. Two sons of his remained behind, and were extremely industrious, taking every opportunity to keep their farm in order, notwithstanding its being in the vicinity of the hostile parties. They were so successful and so little disturbed by the British, that the Americans began to suspect that they were on too good terms with the enemy. Their father's character increased the suspicion. One day, as it subsequently appeared, one of the sons who was working with a wheel plough in cutting his furrows, would every few minutes approach a fence which was between him and the enemy. After several turns as he was making his last cut across the field, he felt his hands suddenly grasped with violence. Impelled by a natural desire to escape, he jumped forwards, and seizing his plough cleaver, he turned at his antagonist, who was an Indian, and felled him to the ground. But a second approached, and with equal dexterity and nerve, he dealt a second blow, which levelled the savage. Both were stunned, their heads being too obvious to escape the terrible blow of the plough cleaver. As they lay on the ground, he alternately struck them over their heads with all his might, and then setting his horses clear from the plough, he ran to the fort and told there what had happened. His tale was not believed, and when he offered to lead them to the spot, they suspected further treachery. They detained him to abide the event, and sent out a detachment to ascertain how the fact was: and these found two savages lying dead at the place he mentioned. This brave feat procured the release of the father, and indeed rescued the whole family from the imputation of toryism forever.

But to return to our domestic movements. Our family was once more reinstated on the farm. We cut the grain that had been left in some of the fields untouched, and foddered our cattle on it during the winter. My poor mother was quite unhappy at the loss of our doors and windows, and the sad ruin

discoverable in everything which a selfish or reck-
less soldiery could convert into fuel, or carry off on
either side.   Still it was our home, and there with
> " Content, our constant guest,"

we were happy for a while in the social connections
of a family, tenderly attached to each other, and in
the cheerful pursuit of avocations to which we had
long been accustomed, and which had ever been
the means of rewarding us with health, peace and
competence.

CHAPTER XXVII.

DURING the winter, notwithstanding the utter annihilation of any thing like a regular and effective force by the capture of Burgoyne, yet the country was considered liable to the incursions of small parties of the enemy. Among other things the church at Saratoga was occupied as a public depot, and the commissary in addition had it partitioned off inside and lived in it. Many a time have I seen barrels of pork and beef rolled in at the sacred porch, which so often had been proclaimed the gate of Heaven. One of the evils of war is the preversion of the most sacred things to the necessities of the moment. In Boston the famous Old South Church was converted into a riding school by the British officers. A church in New York was made a prison for our sick and captured countrymen. The conversion of the church at Saratoga into a commissary's store was the only instance within my knowledge of a similar voluntary abuse by the Americans. During the same winter General Schuyler had twenty four men who were called his life guard constantly in attendance at his residence;

and if I am right in my recollection, during the remainder of the war.

The winter passed away without incident, save one or two feats of skill as a huntsman, shown by my father. He loved to range the woods with his rifle in hand, and all who ever knew him gave him great applause for his dexterity. One evening during this time of quiet he had been induced to set a wolf trap in consequence of some suspicious tracks in the snow, and certain sounds which made our hill sides vocal. In the morning we went out to ascertain the result. Behold! a stout wolf was in the trap, and when we approached he cowed before us, evidently aware of his own defenceless situation. My father succeeded at some risk in muzzling him, and I joyously lifted up trap, wolf and all on my shoulders, and walked off home with them to the great amusement of all who saw me. But this was the first and last ride of the wolf on any body's back. He was condemned to death, and after a short respite, rather for the benefit of our curiosity than to give him any chance of escape, he was placed in a proper position, and at the first fire fell dead on the trap.

In the spring following these events we went down to Bethlehem and brought home our cattle that had wintered there. As we were driving them

slowly back, and as we entered Albany on our
return, we met in State street a procession of novel
character moving slowly up the hill. We perceived
seven persons dressed in white, and soon learned
they were of that unfortunate class of disaffected
men, who to bad political principles had added
crimes against society, which even a state of war
would not justify. At Schodack they had distinguished themselves by a series of desperate acts not
to be patiently endured by the community, and
when they were taken prisoners their fate seemed
inevitable. These men had been confined for some
time in the city prison, afterwards known as the
Old Museum, and had once made their escape, but
only to enjoy their liberty for a few hours. Indeed
the whole city was under arms when we saw them
moving to the fatal spot where they were to suffer.
The public indignation was also much excited by
their conduct in prison, and the circumstances
attending their being brought to suffer the sentence
of the law. They were confined in the right hand
room of the lower story of the prison. The door
of their appartment swung in a place cut out lower
than the level of the floor. When the sheriff came
to take them out he found the door barricaded.
He procured a heavy piece of timber, with which
he in vain endeavored to batter down the door,

although he was assisted in the operation by some very athletic and willing individuals. During the attempt the voice of the prisoners were heard threatening death to those who persevered in the attempt, with the assertion that they had laid a train of powder to blow up themselves and their assailants. Indeed it was well ascertained that a quantity of powder had passed into their possession, but how, could not be known.

It was afterwards found placed under the floor and arranged to produce the threatened result. The sheriff could not effect his entrance, while a crowd of gazers looked on to see the end of this singular contest. Some one suggested the idea of getting to them through the ceiling, and immediately went to work to effect a passage by cutting a hole through. While this was going on the prisoners renewed their threats, with vows of vengeance speedy, awful and certain. The assailants, however, persevered, and as I was informed, and never heard contradicted, procured a fire-engine, and placed it so as to introduce the hose suddenly to the hole in the ceiling, and at a signal inundated the room beneath. This was dexterously performed. The powder and its train were in an instant rendered useless. Still, however, to descend was the difficulty, as but one person could do so at a time. The disproportion of physical strength that apparently awaited the first intruder, prevented for some time any further attempt. At last an Irishman, by the name of Mc-Dole, who was a merchant, exclaimed, "Give me an Irishman's gun, and I will go first." He was provided instantly with a formidable cudgel, and with this in his hand he descended, and at the same moment in which he struck the floor, he levelled the prisoner near him, and continued to lay about him valiantly until the room was filled with a strong party of citizens who came to his assistance through the hole in the ceiling. After a hard struggle they were secured, and the door which had been barricaded by brick taken from the fire-place was opened.

They were almost immediately taken out for execution, and the mob was sufficiently exasperated to have instantly taken their punishment into their own hands. The prisoners seemed to me when moving up the hill to wear an air of great gloom and ill nature. No one appeared to pity them, and their own hopes of being released by some fortunate circumstance, as by the intervention of the enemy, was now banished forever.

They arrived in a few minutes at the summit of the hill, near or at the very place now covered with new and elegant edifices, north and east of the

Academy, and there upon one gallows of rude construction they ended their miserable lives together. This scene is indelibly impressed upon my memory. What I saw I can vouch for, and I believe the circumstances I have related are correct. The transaction created great excitement, and was considered by the Tories as a cruel and unnecessary waste of life, and a sacrifice to the unnatural feelings which had dictated the unhappy rebellion. By the Whigs it was considered as a necessary example demanded by the nature of the times and the enormity of the offences they had committed, and they considered it not only a justifiable, but an imperious necessity to inflict upon the offenders the full penalties of the law. We witnessed the execution, and then set out for home.

CHAPTER XXVIII.

HAVING returned home, we continued our agricultural labors with unceasing diligence. During the season we were continually harrassed by alarms — our days were filled with care, and our nights were passed in anxiety. A part of the First New York (Van Schaick's) regiment, if I remember right, was sent for our protection. The troops were under the immediate command of Lieutenant Colonel Van Dyke. Colonel Van Schaick was in command at Albany, and not in the field. A cancer in his face, which was in consequence of a wound received in the French war, confined him at this time to garrison duty. He always sincerely regretted this misfortune, not so much for its personal inconvenience, as on account of its obliging him to be sometimes absent from his regiment. This gentleman I well knew. He had at an early period made the camp his school; and at the age of nineteen he was appointed a lieutenant by Sir Jeffrey Amherst, who was the personal friend of his father, the then mayor of Albany. He went through his full proportion of active and dangerous service during the celebrated expedition of that general. When the revolutionary war commenced, and the first Albany militia were called out to organize, there was a general request made to him by the citizens of Albany to take command of them and direct the drill. When the New York regiment was raised he received the command with universal approbation. He was ordered by General Schuyler to take command of Fort George in 1775. He was present at the battle of Monmouth, one of the most warmly contested actions of the revolution. His subsequent command was at Fort Schuyler in 1778, when it was in constant danger. His conduct in his expedition at the head of five hundred men into the Indian country, which I shall again allude to, crowned with the most complete success, and without the loss of a single man, has always been considered a masterly movement, and by none more so than by those who were with him and witnessed his soldierlike movements. He was also commanding officer at Albany in 1779. A patriot as well as a soldier, he often supplied the wants of his men from his private purse to his own injury.[1] Many testimonials of high respect and consideration coming from the first men of those times are yet preserved in his family. He was promoted at

[1] See appendix.

the close of the war to the rank of brigadier, with the public approbation of Washington.

During this summer Colonel Quackenboss, of the quartermaster's department, came up to Saratoga with boats and proper equipments to search for cannon, which Burgoyne was supposed to have sunk in the river between Saratoga falls and our farm. My father assisted on this occasion. The sight was a picturesque one. A little squadron of boats well manned, and communicating with the quartermaster general every few minutes, gave life and animation to the scene. The search proved fruitless, no cannon rewarded their toil. One of the men in the boat, of which my father was captain, discovered that his pole touched something round and large. Every eye was stretched to look at it as the water was not deep at the spot. In a few moments several men were stripped and wading about the supposed treasure, and the proper ropes soon adjusted. It was hauled up into the bateau, and proved to be a barrel of smoked hams of the best quality, and not injured in the least, being packed in a tight vessel. They were carried to the house for further examination. One of them was prepared for our dinner, but some of the family were very much afraid of eating it. Burgoyne's hams were thought as hostile as his troops; and they considered it a hazardous attempt to eat what might have been poisoned.   At dinner it was served up, and when Colonel Quackenboss had eaten of it, and was told it was one of Burgoyne's hams, his knife and fork dropped from his hands.   However, the ham was soon demolished, and the gratification of the eaters was not diminished by any further alarms as to its quality.   Before I dismiss the subject of the cannon I ought to mention that a militia captain from Schenectady, by the name of Clute, while swimming near the very same place, the same summer, discovered a small brass howitzer.   With the aid of some of the neighboring farmers he had it drawn on terra firma, and found that his prize was valuable.   He immediately sold it to the government for a handsome sum, and it was forthwith dragged to the barracks.

One of our neighbors, a Colonel Van Vechten, who lived about three miles below the barracks, had a narrow escape about the same time.   He was in the habit of riding from his own house up to General Schuyler's and to the barracks, in order to receive and communicate intelligence.   Those acquainted with the road well remember the ravine and creek just before you reach the church.   In this ravine, concealed behind the trees, a Tory placed himself to shoot Van Vechten as he passed, who had rendered himself obnoxious to the partisans of the English, by his constant assiduity in the service of his country. As he approached, mounted on his favorite grey, the assassin raised his gun to fire. His finger was on the trigger, when, as he afterwards confessed, the bold and manly air which Van Vechten possessed, joined to his unsuspecting manner, unnerved his arm. The weapon of death fell from its position, and Colonel Van Vechten rode by unharmed. It so happened, however, that an alarm which was given while he was at Saratoga in relation to a body of Indians and Tories who had arrived in the neighborhood, induced him to take the river road on his way home, and to give it the preference always afterwards. I mention this anecdote to show the individual danger incurred in those times in particular places, which seemed in no way to subside with the removal of the seat of war.

CHAPTER XXIX.

I CANNOT omit on this occasion to avail myself
of the opportunity offered by circumstances of a
peculiar kind, of relating in detail the particulars of
Colonel Van Schaick's expedition against the Onondagas, derived from a source which I know to be
correct, and by access to private papers of a most
interesting kind. My readers may put full confidence in the narrative.

As I have already mentioned, the defeat of Burgoyne did not free the frontier of this state from
the most harrassing alarms. Sir John Johnson and
the famous Brant, assisted by the Senecas and the
upper nations, were constantly, during this year
and the following, engaged in the detestable pursuit
of plunder, in firing settlements, in taking scalps,
and murdering defenceless women and children.
So complete was the terror excited by their movements that at one time our disheartened citizens
were on the point of abandoning their homes forever. In the words of Colonel Van Schaick, in an
official letter to General Washington, " Schenectady,
under present circumstances, must inevitably become

our frontier settlement." The expeditions of General Sullivan and General James Clinton, one of the bravest and most resolute of soldiers, had their effect in one quarter, while that of Colonel Van Schaick was also productive of the best consequences in another. The Onondagas had become so faithless as to act in alliance with the English, and from their position were of immense detriment to our cause. On the morning of the 19th April, 1779, Fort Schuyler was a scene of busy preparation. After long continued inaction, which was only interrupted by partial skirmishes between our foragers and the Indians that continually hung about the fort, orders were given to the men to prepare for their departure. It was an early hour, while the fog and grey mist of the morning in some measure concealed their movements, that the detachment sallied forth, consisting of 558 men, including officers. Colonel Van Schaick, the gallant Marinus Willett, then lieutenant colonel and Major Cochran, were the field officers of the detachment. They were accompanied by 29 bateaux, into which were placed provisions for eight days, and which were on the previous night cautiously and skillfully removed over the carrying place into Wood creek. A sufficient number of soldiers with five officers were left in charge with them to assist the bateau men and hurry them on. The others pushed on smartly to the old scow place, as it was called, twenty-two miles by land from the fort. They reached this place at three o'clock in the afternoon, but the distance being greater by water, the boats did not all arrive until 10 o'clock at night. Indeed, the numerous obstructions offered by the trees which had fallen into the creek were of themselves very formidable difficulties, overcome only by the determined spirit of the men. As soon as the boats reached the place of rendezvous the troops were all instantly embarked, and the flotilla moved toward Oneida lake. Once in the night the boats in front were ordered to lie too while those in the rear came up. A cold dreary head wind made their progress slow and tedious, but the oars were plied with unremitting diligence. It was not until eight o'clock in the morning that they arrived in Desser's bay, where the bateaux were again to rendezvous. The detachment then moved forward with as much expedition as possible for the Onondaga landing at the head of the lake and opposite old Fort Brewerton, where they arrived at three o'clock P. M. The boats were then left at that place under a proper guard, and the detachment pushed forward toward the enemy. Nine miles, however, was all the distance achieved during the remainder of the day.

The night was a dark and cold one — the heavens gathered blackness, and the men could fancy without the aid of very lively imaginations, that the woods teemed with savages, ready to fall upon them. Indeed, the movements of the hostile Indians, aided by powerful bands of Tories and refugees under the command of Johnson and Brant, had been marked by such fatal celerity, as to leave room for apprehension at every assailable point throughout the western wilderness. The troops, therefore, lay on their arms all night, and were not permitted to light their evening fires. Silently were the watches kept, and with but few words the wearied soldier partook of his evening meal. Silence and secrecy were indeed indispensible to the success of the expedition, and the soldier of two wars, who was responsible for its success, made every arrangement with judgment.

Early the next day, as soon as it was practicable to proceed, the detachment moved on to the Salt lake, since so celebrated for the villages that adorn its shores, the wealth poured into the coffers of individuals, and for its salines more precious than mines of gold. At nine o'clock they reached an arm of the lake. This was forded at a place where the distance was two hundred yards across, and the depth of the water was for most of the distance four

feet. The men, however, marched in good order
through, and pushed on with redoubled speed to
the Onondaga creek. Here it was that a warrior
of that celebrated tribe was captured by Captain
Graham, who commanded a light infantry company.
He was the first Indian discovered, and was instantly
taken. Had he escaped the result of the expedition would have been somewhat uncertain. At this
point it was that arrangements were made to effect
a complete surprise. Captain Graham was ordered
on in advance to attack the nearest settlement of
the Indians only two miles distant, while the old colonel hurried his men by companies as fast as they could
cross a creek on a log (which fortunately served as
a bridge), where the stream was not fordable. One
by one the troops passed over in safety. The circumstance of this log remaining in its place over
the stream is a remarkable one; it was of immense
service, and obviated the delay of seeking a place
to ford at a critical moment. It was the redman's
Thermopylæ. On this occasion a few could have
kept off our troops, for a time at least, which might
have enabled their warriors to rally if not to defeat
the expedition. It allowed the commander to get
into the heart of the enemy's country before they
were apprised of his coming. The careless shout-
ing of soldiers on similar occasions, and the heed-

less discharge of fire arms would have led the wary
and powerful Onondagas to a knowledge of their
impending danger.

The advance of Captain Graham could, however,
be no longer concealed, when in the vicinity of the
castle he was employed in making prisoners. When
the whole detachment arrived at this place, which
was the principal town, situated in the hollow, and
was large and well peopled, the alarm spread. Concealment of their purpose was no longer possible.
The Indians gave away on all sides, making for the
woods. Colonel Van Schaick then dispatched different parties by different routes to get in the rear
of their other settlements, which were scattered
over in different directions eight miles, and they
were ordered to move on with the greatest dispatch.
The alarm spread, however, in spite of every previous precaution, but such was the haste in which
they fled, and such was the ardor with which they
were pursued, that they had not time to carry off a
single article. Thirty-three savages were captured
and twelve killed in the melee. One white man
was also taken prisoner. The whole of their settlements were destroyed, and upwards of fifty of their
best houses burned. A large quantity of corn and
beans was also given to the flames. A hundred
English muskets, a few rifles and some uncommonly

fine horses, together with other animals, were among the booty. Hard as was the task, and severe the punishment, yet it was judged necessary to put the cattle to death, and the horses were shot without hesitation. This act of severity was a blow which the Onondagas long remembered. A considerable quantity of ammunition was found at the council house. After the men had loaded themselves with as much spoil as they could carry, the residue was doomed to destruction and

" The wide field, a waste of ruin made."

The detachment then drew off and commenced their return. In crossing the creek, however, a party of Indians, who had arrived there during their absence, fired upon them unexpectedly from the opposite side. Lieutenant Evans was ordered to beat them off with his riflemen, which he effected in very gallant style without any loss.

The weather, during this day, was propitious. The next day the troops reached the place, and, finding their boats in good order, sailed to the Seven-mile island, where the troops encamped, and had time to rest themselves after their great fatigue. A more picturesque bivouac never was witnessed. The lake was quiet. Its calmness was in keeping with the hour, the gratification of success and the anxiety for repose. The evening fires threw their blaze of light over the waters, and communicated warmth and comfort to the sleeping groups around. There was one who surveyed the scene with unmingled satisfaction. He had accomplished the desirable object for which he had been selected, and by a bold stroke had broken down the strength of the most powerful tribe of all the Indian nations. Numerous and warlike, they had filled the country with alarm, and the cabins of the white men with blood. It was the opinion of General Schuyler, that had not something been done at this crisis we should not have had a settlement beyond Schenectady. Nor were the emotions which belonged to the hour, those of the more obvious feelings of conquest. The recollection that all had been accomplished without the loss of a single man was a source of pleasure that surpassed the excitement of pride and the flush of victory. The next day the detachment crossed the lake and landed two miles from the mouth of Wood creek, at two o'clock in the afternoon, and while two companies were left to guard the bateau men in their navigation up the creek, the remainder of the detachment marched eight miles further and encamped for the night on the banks of Fish creek. The next day several showers of rain impeded their progress to the fort, but notwithstanding, the troops arrived there at noon, after an absence of five days, and a journey of 180 miles.

The thanks of congress were voted to Colonel Van Schaick on this occasion, and to his brave companions, to whom, in his official report, he declared he was "under peculiar obligations" for their cheerfulness "throughout a severe and laborious march, and for the truly determined spirit" shown by them on the occasion.

CHAPTER XXX.

IT was but a short time after Colonel Van Schaick's expedition that the Oneidas appeared in all the pomp and circumstance of an embassy at the fort, to enquire into the reasons of the expedition, and perhaps with secret instructions from the Onondagas, to threaten or conciliate the Americans, as circumstances should permit. Their orator was Priest Peter, as he was then called; and the famous Skenandoah, the principal sachem, was present. The interpreter, Mr. Dean, followed the speaker with these words:

"Brother, you see before you some of your friends, the Oneidas; they come to see you. The engagements that have been entered into between us and our brothers, the Americans, are well known to you.

"We were much surprised, a few days ago, by the news which a warrior brought to our castle with a war shout, informing us that our friends, the Onondagas, were destroyed.

"We were desirous to see you on this occasion, as they think you might have been mistaken in destroying that part of the tribe.

"We suppose you cannot answer us upon this subject, as the matter was agreed upon below. But perhaps you may know something of this matter.

"When we heard of this account we sent back word to our friends remaining among them, telling them not to be pale hearted because some of them were destroyed, but to keep up with their former engagements.

"We sent off some of our people to Canasaraga, to invite them to our village, but they returned an answer that they had sent some of their own runners to Onondaga to learn the particulars, and they waited for their return.

"Our people brought for answer, that they were much obliged to their children, the Oneidas, for attending to them in their distresses, and they would be glad if they would speak smoothly to their brethren, the Americans, to know whether all this was done by design or by mistake.

"If it was a mistake, say they, we hoped to see our brethren, the prisoners—if by design, we still will keep our engagements with you, and not join the king's party. But if our brethren, the Americans, mean to destroy us also, we will not fly — we will wait here and receive our death.

"Brother, this was the answer of the Onondagas. As for us, the Oneidas and Tuscaroras, you know our sentiments. We have supposed we knew yours.

"The commissioners promised us that when they found any thing wrong they would tell us and make it right.

"Brother, if we have done any thing wrong, we shall now be glad if you will now tell us so."

The grunt of the sachems echoed back their approbation to the speaker, as he gracefully threw his mantle over his arm and sat down.

Colonel Van Schaick then arose, and stepping forward, replied as follows:

"I am glad to see my friends, the Oneidas and Tuscaroras. I perfectly remember the engagements the Five nations entered into four years ago, and that they promised to preserve a strict and honorable neutrality during the present war, which was all we asked them to do for us.

"But I likewise know that all of them, except our brethren, the Oneidas and Tuscaroras, broke their engagements and flung away the chain of friendship.

"But the Onondagas have been great murderers; we have found the scalps of our brothers at their castle.

"They were cut off, not by mistake, but by design. I was ordered to do it — and it is done.

"As for the other matters of which you speak, I

recommend a deputation to the commissioners at Albany. I am not appointed to treat with you on those subjects.

"I am a warrior — my duty is to obey the orders which they send me."

My readers will perceive that the answer was as judicious as the appeal had been artful.

The next season the troops at Saratoga were ordered to move to Albany, and I was once more employed in assisting them to remove. Prepared with a good lunch and recommended to the colonel's protection, I fell in as near him as my baggage wagon was permitted, which did not suit the ideas of the wagon master. Why this petty tyranny was exercised over me I never knew, but he endeavored to throw me out the line by every manœuvre that his abilities were equal to. One morning, after vexing me by every means in his power, he came near enough to me to enable me to retaliate, and I lost no time in executing my intention. One of the horses which I drove had been taught to rear, whenever commanded to do so in the name of congress. As the wagon master approached, I cried out, "Do you exercise your authority in name of congress?" giving the sound its usual emphasis. In an instant the sagacious animal reared up and struck my persecutor a blow with his fore feet which sent him

20

staggering away, and left me for some hours in peace and quietness.

It was on our way down when we reached the place now . known by the name of Gibbonsville,[1] where we waited the crossing of the troops who had marched down on the east side of the river, for we had crossed the sprout of the Mohawk, I observed the infliction of corporeal punishment. One of the men who had disobeyed some particular order was struck by his commanding officer, a Capt. Leonard B. The soldier resisted, and defended himself quite valiantly with his musket. Capt. B. lost all command of himself, and snatching the gun out of the man's hand, beat him about the head until the soldier sank to the ground. It excited the universal indignation of the men. Indeed I am confident that the punishment neither benefited the delinquent nor any of his comrades. The universal experience of military men will testify to the truth of my remark.

At one of our stopping places my budget of eatables was placed, at the request of Colonel Van Dyke, on his table, and we partook of it together, with great satisfaction. I mention this merely as a

---

[1] This village in the town of Watervliet, six miles above Albany, and opposite the city of Troy, is not now known as Gibbonsville, but was in 1836 incorporated under the name of West Troy.

trait of the times, and of the little regard paid to the mere distinction of rank. At the crossing of our troops before mentioned, some of us got permission to go on ahead for a few miles towards Albany, where we were to await the arrival of the regiment.

CHAPTER XXXI.

W E then proceeded onward to the buttonwood tree, two miles from Albany, well known at that day for the delightful shade it afforded to the heated traveler. Here our horses were well washed and cleaned, and the same operation we performed on ourselves. By and by, my enemy, the wagon master, came down the road on a *continental* horse without the equipage of an equestrian, but with the ensigns of authority. He brought a guard with him, and we were arrested on the spot. Mortified at this, but aware that we should be revenged, we waited patiently until the regiment came along, when we complained to the colonel. We were instantly liberated, while the wagon-monster, accoutred as he was, received a pointed rebuke, and was disgraced before the whole line.

The troops entered the city in handsome style, drums beating and colors flying. They were marched to the hill and there encamped. We were next dismissed, and we endeavored to get our friend, the wagon-master, to return with us in the wagons, as he intended to go back. We concealed under this invitation our intention to give him a basting for his previous conduct to us. He did not accept our offer, but withdrew himself out of our way as soon as possible.

In the beginning of 1780 we were employed in drawing boards and provisions to Fort Anne. It is well known that an expedition was contemplated against Canada in the preceding year, and, if I remember right, Gen. Lafayette, who was expected from France early in this year, was to have had the command. Indeed the plan of operations is fully detailed by Marshall. Fort Anne was then nothing but a rough block house with a picket around it. It had, however, been distinguished for several gallant actions performed before and within its precincts. It was one thing to be *employed* by congress, and another thing to be *paid* by them. It was our fortune on this occasion, as on former ones, to know the difference: we *drew* the *boards* but never *drew* our *pay*.

While we held undisturbed possession of the posts at the north, it was a very common thing for the different commanders to exchange visits. Colonel Warner of Fort Edward occasionally visited Fort George. On one of these occasions he was returning with two officers, all of them mounted on horseback. As they were passing the bloody pond, where some hostile Indians had hid themselves behind an old tree, they received a volley of musketry from their concealed enemies. The two officers fell lifeless to the ground, and Colonel Warner was wounded, as was the horse he rode. He put spurs to the bleeding animal and endeavored to escape. One of the officers' horses followed him and the Indians pursued. As he rode on his horse occasionally seemed ready to fall under him, and at other times would revive and appear to renew his strength. The other horse kept up with them, alternately increasing and relaxing his speed to keep pace with his wounded companion. The colonel in vain endeavored to seize the bridle which hung over his neck, an expedient which promised to save him if his own steed should fail. In this manner, and with all the horrid anticipation of a cruel death before him, he managed to outstrip his pursuers until he reached Wing's corner at Glen's falls. There, as the uninjured horse came along side, he made another attempt to seize his bridle, and succeeded. He instantly dismounted, unslung the saddle, threw it over the fence, mounted the horse and rode off at full speed. He saw no more of his pursuers from this moment, but reached Fort Edward in safety; overcome, however, by his exertion, fatigue, and the loss of blood. What was also singular, was the arrival of his wounded horse, which lived to do good service in the field.

The individual suffering of our western brethren was never greater than at this time. I was so situated as to observe many circumstances of the kind alluded to, and the flight of some of our relatives from Schoharie to my father's house at this time was the reason why many anecdotes connected with the incursions of the savages are remembered with facility. The harvests were never more promising than at this time, and, for the sake of obtaining food for their suffering families, the people of Schoharie returned to remain on their farms almost among the last. There were block houses near the settlements, to which, in case of alarm, the inhabitants fled, and, as a part of the system of defence, they in turns went out as scouts, in order to discover any threatened danger, and to give the alarm. On the morning of the day which Schoharie will long remember, John Vrooman, well known as *old rifle*, and two others were out upon duty. They were in the woods, about eight miles distant from the settlement, anxiously reconnoitering every suspicious object, and ready to fight or fly, as was most necessary, when Vrooman caught a glance of an Indian, who appeared engaged in a business similar to their own. "See there," cried he to his

companions, "there is one of the black devils, as I
live!" The next instant he raised his rifle to his
face, and with a rashness that he afterwards rued,
he fired and the savage fell. Another Indian discovered himself, and Vrooman's companion fired
at him. This one also fell, apparently dead. A
third rose, as if to give them each a chance of firing,
but the third scout became alarmed at this third
vision, and refused to fire. Vrooman snatched the
rifle from his hand, and shot this one also. Instantly
a group of Indians and Tories rose from the ground
near them with a yell, and in a manner that clearly
indicated that they were disturbed in finishing their
breakfast. "Did you see that flock of crows?"
said Vrooman, "we shall have a warm day of it,
let every one take care of himself!"

He was an old woodsman, and as the three scouts
separated he immediately made a tack and dashed
into the thickest of the forest. The enemy pursued him, and it was only by a series of zig-zag
flights that he reached the fort at Vrooman's flats
at noon, breathless, exhausted, and completely worn
out by fatigue. He was scarcely there before the
flames of the dwellings at the settlement were visi-
ble. Brant at the first alarm pushed for the
settlement, by an old road, and was already doing
his work of devastation.

CHAPTER XXXII.

I HAD an aunt living at the place, whose husband, at the moment of Brant's arrival, was engaged in loading his barn with hay, and was himself on the load with the pitchfork in his hand, while his sons were in the barn stowing it away. As he accidently looked around he discovered the Indians between him and the house. At the same instant he heard his wife scream. He had presence of mind, however, to cry out, "My boys, the enemy!" He jumped from the load with the apparent intention of making for the cornfield. As he struck the fence a ball went through him, and he fell dead on the spot. His wife was coming out of the garden, where she had just parted with a female friend, a neighbor, when she saw the savages, and gave the shriek which had alarmed her husband. The wretches seemed dead to all the claims of sex or age, and she was instantly tomahawked. The three oldest of the sons were made prisoners, while the youngest brother, of about five years of age, who had been playing about the wagon in the field, came running to the house. At the sight of his mother weltering in her blood, he gave away to agony of grief, and screamed as loud as his voice permitted. For a moment they endeavored to stop his cries, but not succeeding in their attempt to pacify him, they knocked him on the head also, and he fell at the door by the side of his unfortunate mother. Thus, in a few moments, with circumstances of hellish barbarity, was a family put to a cruel and savage death. The three captives were carried away to Canada. They did not obtain their liberty until nearly two years afterwards. I well remember their return. My father obtained information of it, and went to the north to meet them. He brought them home to his own house, and there learned the story of their sufferings and exile. From their long captivity, and their continued labors in the field without hats, both in the service of the savages and the Canadians, they were burned very black, and presented a woful appearance.

It was during the same incursion that, as the wife of John Vrooman was alone in her house, an Indian by the name of Hendrik, a Mohawk, who had lived near Schoharie, and knew all the inhabitants, came in. As he entered the dwelling his eyes were attracted by a brown coat which hung up there. "Whose coat is that?" said he. On being told by her with a trembling voice, he replied, "If the owner were here, he would never wear another." Both she and her mother were carried off and kept one night in duress. The ensuing morning they were sent back by the ferocious Brant, and were the bearers of a letter written on birch bark, explaining his reasons for so doing.

The Vrooman family were peculiarly unfortunate. One of its members, by the name of Ephraim, ran into his house to get his gun and powder horn, determined to sell his life as dearly as he could; but as he was in the act of taking them from the wall where they hung, he was clenched by a savage who followed him in, and was made prisoner. This was not less aggravating from witnessing the unavailing attempt made by his wife to escape at the same moment. She darted towards the road, where the ground descended rapidly, and where she hoped to have got out of their sight. She was shot dead ere she reached the road. Nor is this all. A daughter whom she fondly loved, of the age of eleven years, had laid hold of her clothes, and ran with her. An Indian came up to them, and observing the child lying close to her mother, as if seeking her protection, he snatched up a stone from the ground and dashed out her brains. Such were some of the incidents of that horrid scene.

Some of the inhabitants, however, escaped under circumstances very extraordinary, and worthy of reminiscence. The road which led from the upper to the middle fort ran across the hill. At the time of the enemy's approach two men were in the field with a wagon and horses, busily engaged in work. They were at least two miles and a half from the fort. They heard the noise of the engagement, and instantly attempted to escape. One of them stood up and drove, while the other, with his pitch-fork, goaded the horses to their topmost speed. No less than seven swing-gates interposed themselves, as barriers on the road, but, as most miraculously they were made to swing either way, they were forced open by the horses running against them. During this terrible race against time, several persons succeeded in getting into the wagon from behind, and these laid hold of every person who came near enough to attempt the same exploit. As they passed a point where an old person by the name of Swarts resided, who was unloading some corn from a wagon, they gave him the alarm, and being near the goal they wished to arrive at, slackened their pace. He told them not to wait for him. He sent one of his men to his house to call his wife, while he reharnessed his horses to the wagon. His poor wife came running out, the picture of distraction, and in her fright forgot her child, that was sleeping in a cradle. She was surprised at her forgetfulness and ran back for it. The three were then hauled into the wagon as quick as possible. The horses were forced into a gallop down the hill and through the creek. Notwithstanding they were pursued by the savages the whole of the distance, they escaped, reaching the fort in safety, with eleven persons in the wagon, picked up in this singular manner. The harness was covered with clotted blood, and the poor animals were completely exhausted. Another person escaped across the flats in this way. Whenever he found his pursuer gaining on him, he would turn round and point something which he carried towards the savage, as if he was about to fire. This occasioned a halt, and with a fresh breath drawn at those intervals, he completely succeeded in getting safely into the fort.

This excursion cost Schoharie twelve houses burned, and nearly a hundred people massacred and made prisoners. The whole of their labor was lost for the season, and one of the finest crops that ever graced the fertile plains of Schoharie was destroyed. One house, amid this general devastation, escaped from the circumstance of its being the place where treaties had been held on former occasions.

CHAPTER XXXIII.

THIS celebrated excursion, as I before mentioned, was conducted by Sir John Johnson and Brant. The force which they had with them has always been said to have been 1,150, counting red and white. A part of their plan was to have attacked the middle fort at Middleburgh. Many a time and oft, as I have crossed the kil at this place, and sauntered along its pleasant banks, forming, as it were, a natural street for the quiet village, have I looked in vain for the traces of that horrid assault which destroyed the settlement in 1780. Yet there is a stone dwelling house, standing between the hill and the creek, and well known by the appellation of Becker's stone house, which then served as a rallying place for the fugitive settlers, and by the aid of a picket and some minor defences was thought worthy of the title of fort. I might have been a little more systematic in the relation of the events of which I am now reminiscent, but I am sure the excuse of old age will save me from the criticisms of mere chronologists.

The rear of the enemy, while on their march to

the middle fort, was discovered by the lookouts at the upper fort, and immediately three guns were discharged as a signal to the neighborhood.   As I have before mentioned the inhabitants were engaged in their usual business, for they always hoped to be able to retire to the fort before the danger became imminent.   When the alarm was given my grandfather was in the fort, and his son was in a mill which belonged to the family, about one mile from the place.   The former immediately went down to the mill, and the two shut it up and stopt its motion. This was considered very venturesome in the old man, but he was not immediately exposed through his rashness.   Besides, the life of a favorite son was not the least incentive on the occasion.   He and his son mounted two horses that were there, while the miller trusted to his legs for security.   As the fugitives approached the fort on their return they discovered the enemy within a hundred yards of them.   They immediately changed their course, and got in at the rear of the fort without further risk.   This was early in the morning.   After sunrise Sir John Johnson surrounded the middle fort, and sent a flag demanding its surrender.   Exasperated by the sufferings they had already undergone, and perhaps by a knowledge of the mischief already done at the flats, and incited to hostility by the remarks of some old people, that they wanted no

red-coats in the fort, they told the sentry to fire at
the flag and drive it off. A Major W., a continental officer, who was stationed there, endeavored
to prevent this outrage of military etiquette, and
commanded the sentry not to fire. The militia
officer overruled him, and gave peremptory orders
to the man to fire. This dispute was not without
interest. A group of controversialists were assembled on the occasion, and furnished a scene
which the painter might seize on to transfer to his
canvass, worthy of the humorous pencil of Hogarth,
if not rivaling his famous tribute to the hostile
properties of roast beef before the gates of Calais.
I can imagine the moment when the willing sentry,
looking beyond the rude palisade which skirted
the fort, saw the white flag drawing nearer with
that uncertainty of manner which indicates the
doubt of a favorable reception. Raising his musket to his shoulder, he looked around for some
approving look from his comrades in arms. The
distant smoke which he well knew was from the torch
of the incendiary, and the glitter of the red-coats
just within sight of him, gave a sort of tremor to
his hand, and he thought of the fate which perhaps
awaited them all. Just behind him stood the
extremes of continental etiquette and militia subor-
dination, personified in the one instance by a sharp

and huge cocked hat, trimmed profusely with gold lace, surmounting a well powdered head. The lips of the officer firmly set, and his right hand resting on a cane with which he now and then laid down his argument, and somewhat roundly too, on the toes of his unlucky listeners around him. A long waisted blue coat turned up with buff, that met and parted at the same time on his breast, and a black silk kerchief drawn tightly round his throat, completed the upper part of our major. A pair of small clothes drawn tightly over a muscular thigh were met at the knee by a pair of straight sided boots that doubtless by their stiffness and want of pliability prevented any thing like an attack upon the limb inside. A white belt thrown over the whole man, and a heavy sabre with a leathern scabbard completed the Ajax of the council, the son of chivalry and the regularly fed friend of the continental congress. But the nicely drawn arguments taken from the rules of war, and ever and anon supported by the dicta of the Prussian Baron Steuben, who had brought order into the disorderly ranks of our armies, were lost upon the rude minds of his unlettered, but exasperated companions. Their embrowned visages, but illy protected by their ancient hats, which had served at least during war, declared that revenge and an

22

obstinate defence were all they wished, and that
the means which were to lead to these were not
to be invaded by rules to which they, at least, had
never subscribed. Besides, there was a feeling
almost of animosity against congress and the regular army, on account of the indifference with which
their cries for assistance had apparently been heard.
It is well known to those persons who were in the
confidence of General Schuyler and Colonel Van
Schaick that strong and repeated applications for
reinforcements had been denied, though for reasons
imperious in their nature, and such as admitted of
no compromise. It is well known that even a few
barrels of flour and beef which now and then were
dispatched from the magazines in the highlands,
when arrived at Schenectady, laid there for weeks
before a sufficient guard could be mustered to protect it to the river forts. Recollections like these
were not likely to give success to the opinions of
the continental major. In such a group of combatants just escaped from the tomahawk, hastily
equipped for defence, and bearing a grotesque
appearance, the name of Steuben was of no more
weight than the feather which waved in the breeze.

Brown shirts were the panoply of the farmer
soldiers, over them hung powder horns and shot
bags, manufactured during the winter nights, and

now and then stopped up with a corn cob which had escaped the researches of the swinish multitude. Muskets were rather uncommon. Long fowling pieces were more in fashion in Schoharie. Sometimes the rank of the individual led him to greater expense in equipment. A sparse sprinkling of gold lace in places best calculated for display, a long feather and a thin epaulette were indicative of the superior pretensions of the man who wore them.

CHAPTER XXXIV.

OCCASIONALLY in the interstices of the disputants an old man or two would be listening with that peculiar expression of countenance which argues the possession of hard hearing. These, who had generally known something of service in the French war, would occasionally chime in with yes or no, as the controversy came within the range of their memories. There was another argument used, which, after all, was perhaps the most powerful of any; and this was the fact, that however etiquette might be regarded by the besieged, it certainly was not likely to produce a correspondent feeling on the part of the enemy. Already they had experienced the truth of the position, in the murders committed upon the unsuspecting inhabitants, and these, too, after they had surrendered. The savages and their companions the Tories, still more savage than they, had shown no respect to age, sex or condition, and it was with force the question was repeated, "are we bound to exercise a forbearance totally unreciprocated by the enemy? Besides, let us show that we neither give nor take quarter. They will discover our desperation and withdraw." On the whole, the friends of etiquette were overpowered. The order to fire was repeated, and the close shot of the sentinel drove away at full speed the bearer of the flag of truce. The major, however, unwilling to be responsible for the consequences, retired to his pallet, and excused himself from any further command at present, alleging his indisposition. A Captain Vrooman was invested with the honors of the command, and at the head of 350 men, besides women and children, resolved to fight while there was a combatant of either sex left alive. After the violation of the flag Sir John brought up his artillery, and fired upon the fort. The fire was promptly returned. Having a few light howitzers with him, he threw a few shells, of which only two struck the building. One of them entered the roof of a small building in the pickets and fell through the roof into a room where two sick women were lying. It was arrested in its fall by a feather bed, where it exploded and scattered a gale of feathers about the apartment. No serious injury, however, occurred. An effort was made to set fire to the pickets and out houses, by loading a wagon with dry wheat, and after firing it, to shove it as close to the place as possible. This attempt also failed. Either the sharp shooting of the riflemen, or the short lived flames of the material which was used, prevented any injury. The principal part of the day was occupied in operations of this kind, when the sentry again discovered the approach of a white flag. In an instant the news was about, and a crowd again assembled to watch its coming. Major W———, with the rest, determined to make his last stand against the invasion of military law. A Captain Reghtmeyer, however, was on the platform where the soldier stood, and he gave him the order to fire. The major, exasperated at this, drew his sword, and seemed about to run the delinquent through. The little captain, who carried a fusee in his hand, instantly clubbed it, and made an impressive motion with its breech, which again drove the major back to his retreat.

During this petty siege the enemy would draw off their forces, and burn and destroy dwellings in the neighborhood. At these intervals our men would succeed in killing numbers of them, but the moment any thing like a show of force took place, the latter would run back, repass the gate under the protection of a heavy fire from their comrades, and the small artillery, within the walls. During this desultory warfare, which lasted from morning to night, the females within our fort displayed a heroism worthy of commemoration. They were well provided with arms, which they intended to use if the English attempted to take the place by storm. Their services were not required by such an extremity.   One of these, then an interesting and handsome young female, whose name is still mentioned with respect by the people of Schoharie, displayed a good deal of courage on this occasion.   Perceiving that one of our men, who went to draw water from a well within reach of the enemy's fire, scudded into the fort as fast as he could to escape it, she gallantly went out herself and drew water for the men in the fort as long as any was required. Without changing color, she carried bucket after bucket to the thirsty combatants, and providentially she escaped without the slightest injury.

Finding the fort too strong for them, the enemy drew down to the lower fort, and after skirmishing until sundown, without much effect, drew off towards the Mohawk river.   By this time, however, the alarm had spread through the neighboring settlements, and a body of militia of sufficient force to become the assailants, arrived, it is said, within a short distance of the enemy near the river, and Sir John Johnson, in consequence, had actually made arrangements to surrender.   The Americans, however, at this moment, fell back a short distance, for the sake of occupying a better position during the night.   The interval was improved by the enemy, and by great exertions on their part, floats and rafts were constructed, upon which they passed over before the Americans came up in the morning. There is a tradition among the Schoharie people, however, that as the last float was going over, a British officer who was on it, offered a fair mark for the rifle, in consequence of the glitter of his dress in the light of the morning sun. A friendly Oneida asked permission to fire at him, and on its being given, he took a rest for his rifle in order to take a good aim, fired and shot the officer instantly.

CHAPTER XXXV.

I THINK it was upon this occasion that Governor George Clinton, to whose indefatigable exertions the state of New York owes more than she could repay, ordered out the militia of the different counties, and at their head proceeded to the northward, in hopes to cut off the retreat of the enemy. With the greatest activity his men were collected and dispatched to Lake George. No tidings being gained of them, however, the governor determined to proceed, and having boats at Caldwell, he prepared to embark for Ticonderoga. It so happened that my father was selected to take charge of the barge in which the governor embarked. He immediately made a selection of the best oarsmen he could find, and all being ready the flotilla moved to the lake. Is was a doubtful voyage. The governor was one of those men, who, not at all elevated by the high dignity and responsibility of his station, knew how to please every class of citizens by making himself cheerful and familiar. They had a fine passage down the lake. The enemy, however, was not to be found. Governor Clinton then resolved to push on to Crown Point.

23

A scouting party of three men was selected to explore the country. One very intelligent man was chosen, who, among other things, was known for his singularity in refusing to wear shoes. He absolutely refused to go, unless he had permission to go alone. This excited Governor Clinton's curiosity. He requested the man to come to him. He was astonished at the grotesqueness of his appearance, and at first doubted his capacity for the intended business. He enquired why he demanded to go alone. The man replied that his companions *would only have to wait for him* in the woods. He was permitted to adopt his own measures, and was ordered to push ahead for fifteen miles, and return again as soon as possible. He left the governor's head quarters at three in the afternoon, and at half past nine next morning had returned, after having traveled thirty miles during that period, but observed nothing suspicious. It was pretty well ascertained that the enemy had not retreated in that direction, and the governor gave up all hopes of intercepting them on this occasion, and returned home. It was at this time that the governor, pleased with my father's conduct and discretion, told him that he would see him the next day at an hour which he fixed, to converse with him upon a subject of some interest. Unfortunately for me, my father forgot the appointment, for it afterwards turned out that the governor intended to have given me a lieutenant's commission. The delay, however, lost all. After waiting two hours for my father's arrival the governor returned to Albany, and the golden opportunity was lost.

In Saratoga we continued constantly exposed to the harrassing incursions of the Tories and Indians. Almost the whole country was alarmed by them, and with the subtlety peculiar to the savage intellect, they seemed to escape every attempt at capture. Often we have seen them running across the fields upon the opposite side of the river, now stooping behind fences which afforded them a partial cover, and now boldly running across the open ground, where the fences were down, to some other enclosed field, along which they skulked as before. During these alarms our neighbors used to come and live with us for weeks together until the danger was over, and then they would return home. The principal men of the county had guards stationed at their dwellings. Gen. Schuyler had usually twenty-four at his house. Some of the militia colonels who had become obnoxious to the enemy were protected by smaller guards of five and six men about each house. Minor precautions were also taken, and the relation of some of them will show my readers how wearisome was the life we led. My father was in the habit of stacking his corn in the field, and indeed all his grain, placing it as far as possible from the fences, for in case of surprise, and if his dwelling should be burned, he knew what was scattered through the fields would in a measure be safe. It was a common thing in those days for the farmers with us to transport their grain to Albany during the winter, and keep it stored there for protection. In the summer it was carried back load by load, as it was wanted for use.

In the fall alarms still continued, and every precaution, as was usual, was taken by us. We used to stack our straw in the field, near the house, and so erect the pile, as to leave at the top a conical hole, in which two persons kept watch during the alarms, this way, every night. A ladder was placed for us to mount with our guns, and when we were ensconced, it was withdrawn. One slept while the other watched, and though our elevation was not more than ten feet, it gave us a great advantage in detecting the approach of the enemy. Perched in these cyries we passed night after night, while our sleepless eyes strained their vision to catch the least appearance of the foe. Indeed we commanded a full view of the river, and to the north and west for a great distance. Nor was this the only method which caution induced us to take.   The horses were frequently harnessed to our sleds at night, which made, of course, less noise than the wagons, to transport our baggage down to a ravine for the sake of preserving it from an expected incursion.

I well remember when my father was obliged to leave home in company with the neighboring militia, and leave it too, with the impression that it would be burned before he returned to his family. My poor mother has been so alarmed at night, as to hasten, with her children, down to the ravine I have mentioned, and there pass the night in the open air.   In the morning she would cautiously approach the house, scarcely knowing whether it yet afforded a shelter.

These alarms were harassing in the extreme, and they kept us unquiet while the war continued. I will relate one or two circumstances which came within my personal observation, and which will impress my reader with a more lively idea of what we were doomed to undergo.

CHAPTER XXXVI.

ONE Sunday night, after all the family had retired to their bed, it being a still, clear night in the fall of the year, we heard our dogs barking violently in the front of the house, while a confused sound of voices accompanied the deep mouthed baying. In an instant my father was out of bed, and ready for action, when my prudent mother checked his impetuosity by saying, he was not a match for the persons without, that if he went out he would be taken, and that perhaps, if all was kept still within the house, the enemy would not think it necessary to commit any violence, for the sake of securing their own safety, and go off. Gradually the noise of the dogs became fainter and more distant, and before many minutes passed away it was as still and tranquil as ever. It was not long afterwards ascertained, that the cause of the disturbance was the approach to the house of a party of Tories with fire-arms, led on by a fellow by the name of Loveclass. When all was quiet, my father, with his gun in his hand, stole cautiously out of the house, and followed in the direction of the noise when last heard. It led him to the river,

and he had scarce reached the bank, when he distinctly heard the noise of a canoe paddle as it
touched the sides of the sonorous machine.   Every
one who has noticed the sound of the oars of a
boat or the paddles of a canoe will readily recollect
the hollow tone which they make, and which, on
some occasions, has an unnatural effect upon the
ear.   My father, by long use, had become accustomed not only to distinguish these peculiar sounds,
but knew his own canoe by the tones its hollow
trough gave out at the touch of the rower.   On
this occasion his acute ear told him that his canoe
was nearly across the river.   For a moment he
hesitated whether he should not fire in the direction
of the noise, but on reflection he thought the risk
too great, and the advantage too remote to be hazarded by the discharge of his rifle.   Slowly he
turned his back homewards, while his faithful curs
at his first approach, having discovered their master,
followed at his heels with a whine, which almost
spoke their uneasiness and alarm.   In the morning
the canoe was discovered on the other side of the
river, and the circumstances led to suspicion that
all was not right.   My father, as the sequel will
show, had been in great danger, and his neighbors
felt very unpleasantly about it; and Colonel Van
Vechten, our vigilant friend, was constantly on the

alert to discover who those persons could have
been, and whether they were in the vicinity of
Saratoga.   There was a Captain Dunham, who
commanded a militia company in the neighborhood,
a great Whig, and a firm friend of ours, who also
exerted himself to trace the marauder, and was in
frequent consultation with Colonel Van Vechten
on the subject.   One evening, as they were together
at a place of public entertainment, if such a thing
could be such in those times, a boy was seen emerg-
ing from the woods in the neighborhood on horseback, and presently approaching the place where
they were, asked if he could purchase a little rum.
When he was answered, "No," he immediately
mounted, returned a considerable distance, and then
was seen galloping down the main road by the
river side.   On seeing this Dunham exclaimed,
"This means something, I am sure of it!"   They
then watched for the boy's return, and in a few
minutes he repassed at full speed.   He then reën-
tered the wood, and was gone from their sight in
an instant.   Dunham's penetration induced him to
say, "Van Vechten, the enemy is near us; the
Tories are in our neighborhood and not far off."
They separated with a determination to act immediately.

Dunham, when he reached home, immediately

went to a person by the name of Green, who was a son of Vulcan, an able-bodied, bold and persevering fellow. He was the pride of his settlement and the safeguard of the people around him — always ready for action, never desponding, and fearless to an extent that was remarkable. He was always relied upon in trying emergencies by the leading men in the vicinity, and what completed his merit was, he was never dilatory. Dunham related the circumstance to him, and declared his belief that there was a party of Tories in the neighborhood. Three other persons were called upon the same night for their assistance, and when the rest of their neighbors were asleep these hardy men commenced their reconnoissance. Every suspected spot was carefully approached in hopes to observe the objects of their search. Every hollow that could contain a hiding place was looked into; but in a more particular manner the out-houses and barns of those persons who were suspected for their attachment to the enemy were examined by them. It seemed all in vain. No traces of a concealed foe were discovered, when towards daybreak it was proposed to separate and make one final search for that time. Dunham took two men with him, and Green but one. The former, as a last effort, returned to the house of one Odeurman, who, it was probable, would be in communication with an enemy, if near him. As he approached the house he had to pass a meadow adjoining, and observed a path leading from the house to a small thicket of about three acres extent. Dunham immediately suspected it led to his enemy. He pursued it, and found it passed round the thicket, and when it almost met the place where it turned off, the path entered the wood. Dunham paused, and turning to his companions said, "Here they are, will you follow me?" They instantly agreed to accompany him, and the party moved on in single file, with light and cautious steps. As they got nearly to the centre, Dunham in advance, a log stopped up the path, and seemed to prevent any further approach. With a motion that indicated the necessity of their remaining still, he mounted the log, and looking over, discovered, sure enough, at once a desired and yet imposing sight. Round the remains of a watch fire, which day break rendered less necessary, sat a group of five fierce looking men, with countenances relaxed from their usual fixedness, but yet betokening boldness, if not savageness of purpose. They were dressing themselves and putting on their shoes and stockings, which stood by the side of their rude couches. Their clothes were much worn, but had a military cut, which made their stout and muscular forms more apparent, had a peculiar snug fit, and distinguished them from the loose, slovenly, scare crow figures which the homely character of our country seamstresses imposed upon every thing rural or rusticated among our people. Their hats or caps were set carelessly on their heads, with the air of regulars; and what made them still more observable was, that every man of them had his musket at his side on the ground, ready to be used at an instant's notice. Dunham surveyed this scene a few moments, and then drew back cautiously to his companions. In a tone not above a whisper, he said, "*Shall we take 'em ?*" A nod from his companions decided him. Each now examined his musket and reprimed it. The captain took the right of his little band, and they moved forward to the log. They mounted it at the same instant, and, as they did so, Dunham cried out "Surrender, or you are all dead men!" The group that thus found themselves almost under the muzzles of their enemies' guns were indeed astonished. All but their leader, Lovelass, seemed petrified and motionless. This resolute man seemed disposed to make an effort for their lives. Twice amid the silence and stillness of the perilous moment he stretched out his hand to seize his gun. Each time he was prevented by the nearer approach of the muzzle that pointed at his head, and beyond which he saw an unflinching eye steadfastly fixed upon him, at the same instant he was told, that if he touched it he was dead.

At this critical period of the rencontre Dunham peremptorily ordered the party to come out, one by one, which they reluctantly did, fearing, perhaps, that they were surrounded by and in contact with a superior force. As fast as one came over the log he was secured by the most powerful man of the three, while the other two kept their pieces steadily pointed at the other prisoners. In this way they were secured, and were marched out of the thicket to the adjacent house. The inmates of the dwelling were thunderstruck at perceiving the prisoners. Some young women, who proved to be sisters of some of the party, gave way to the most violent grief. Well aware of the danger they were in, and of the speedy vengeance inflicted upon Tories and spies, they anticipated the most dreadful consequences. to their unhappy brothers, and no words can express the frantic sorrow to which they abandoned themselves. The young men themselves assumed an air of firmness, but it was easily penetrated. They were marched off to Saratoga barracks, and as they came up the main road opposite to our house we saw them approach, and my father and myself spoke to them. They confessed that they were the persons who had alarmed us on the night to which I have already alluded.

After crossing in the canoe they had lain two days and nights in the bush, a quarter of a mile from the river, looking out for persons alone, and intending to capture the principal and most active of the neighboring Whigs. They did not deny that they had deliberated some time as to the propriety of taking my father off with them, but as their main attempt was to have been against Colonel Van Vechten, they concluded not to hazard their ultimate object by precipitation.

The poor wretches were tried and condemned at a court martial, of which the celebrated Stark was president. Lovelass alone suffered death. He was considered too dangerous a man to be permitted to escape. He complained that being found with arms in his hands, he was only a prisoner, and many thought, that such being the fact, he was scarcely punishable as a spy. Indeed he even bewailed his hard fate, and the injustice done him, but found he had nothing to expect from the judges. In two or three days he was brought out upon the hill, on the south side of General Schuyler's house, and suffered death upon the gallows. Nothing could have been more quiet and unaffected than his manner; the spectators themselves were touched with compassion, but public policy seemed to require an unbending sternness on the part of the court, and his punishment certainly put an end for that time to all marauding expeditions by the Tories. Lovelass's companions were sent down the river the same day to a depot for prisoners.

CHAPTER XXXVII.

It was about the same time I remember, I had been sent by my father from home a considerable distance, in order to obtain the services of a person wanted as a servant in the family; I did not succeed in the attempt, and was delayed on my return home until dark. When I arrived and had put away my horse, I went into the house, and found my parents gone, and the younger children who were incapable of giving me much information on the subject sitting like statues round the expiring embers of the kitchen fire in solemn and melancholy silence, their countenances expressive of uncertainty if not of dread, and uttering deep drawn sighs, as their eyes wandered round the deserted room. Not knowing the actual reason of their desertion, yet conforming strictly to the commands left with them by their parents, they had scarcely ventured to move from their seats until I came in, and while I was struck with the peculiarity of their behavior, as well as the strangeness of the absence of the family, I bade them remain quiet while I stepped out of the house to see if I could discover any thing. I had scarcely reached the open air when the screaming of a child apparently at a distance down the river, fell upon my ear, and made my blood run cold. "What can this mean!" I exclaimed. The cry continued — My curiosity increased, and hastily seizing a musket, I told the children to remain where they were, and I would return in a few minutes. I shall never forget the imploring, yet checked expression of alarm, which those dear little creatures gave me. I did not wait to hear them say a word, but hastened down to the river. The noise plainly increased, piercing the ear of night. I crossed the road which led down to the ferry, and secreted myself behind a fence, where I thought I could make the most of my concealment, while I caught with breathless anxiety the incessant screams of the child. I soon distinguished the hasty plunging of oars, and in a few moments more, a number of persons landed from a boat just under my feet. Scarcely knowing what was best to do, I cried out, "Who goes there?" I shall never forget the complete felicity I enjoyed on hearing my father's well known reply, "John, is that you, my boy, what are you doing here?" I instantly emerged from my post, and explained the cause of my alarm. I immmediately perceived the party were our friends, consisting of Colonel V., and P., with their families and domestics who were coming up to stay with us on account of the dangers

which were supposed to threaten them at home.
The men had walked along the river side while
their wives came in the boat, rowed by the blacks;
but they were not a little perplexed at the circumstances of the infant of Mrs. V. having most
unaccountably commenced screaming without any
cause. No caresses could stop it, and when alarmed
at being discovered, they tied a pocket handkerchief about its face, they found its lungs too powerful for that. They were very thankful for their
safe arrival. An enemy could have heard the child
cry for two miles, such was the stillness of the night.
We all proceeded in a body up to our dwelling,
which for many weeks resembled a garrison rather
than a house.

While we were all under the effects of the excitement of the evening we were quite unprepared for an
event which took place some few hours after. We had
thirteen guns loaded and in order, and being divided
into watches we stood as sentries round the house.
It soon came my turn to go out with one of the
blacks by the name of Ned, whom on most occasions, a pair of fleet heels served a friendly part.

Rumor *addidit* alas ! Ned however, talked largely
and I felt no backwardness in stating what havoc
we would make among the Tories with our thirteen
guns. While every one was fast asleep, about

25

midnight, during one of our walks towards a fence which ran down to the river, as the moon was just rising behind us and throwing a faint light on the scene beyond, I perceived with horror the approach of objects whose movements appeared to be governed by the most perfect military rules. Every now and then they would halt, and after a short rest would move on with the same precision. They were crossing a wheat-field which lay to the south of the fence I have mentioned, anxious to get under its cover for the purpose of concealing their approach to the house. The rustling of the stubble seemed to be as carefully avoided as possible. I watched them with the deepest interest until they made a deliberate and regular halt when they came to the fence. I was then convinced we were in imminent danger, and turning round to give some order to my companion, found he was gone. I hesitated not a moment to follow his example, and hastening to the house, arrived there about the same time with Ned. We woke up the sleepers with the startling information that a large number of disciplined men were within a quarter of a mile of the house and approaching it with caution and perfect regularity.

In an instant all the men were armed and ready. My father volunteered to run down a few rods and

reconnoitre. He did so, and came back with the
news that they were coming. A brief consultation
was held as to the best manner of receiving them,
as flight was impracticable under the circumstances
without abandoning both wives and children. One
was for firing as they mounted a fence that went
across at right angles to the house parallel to the
river. Another was for opening upon them as
they ascended the rising ground that intervened
between the house and bank of the river. The last
project was approved, and we were cautioned to fire
low, and to make every shot tell. The party stationed themselves accordingly and I then volunteered to go down and take another look. They
still appeared in motion, but apparently without
caution approached the bank and fence running
parallel to it. There they halted for some time,
and I hastened back with the intelligence. Their
apparent irresolution inspired us with fresh vigor,
and we began to grow more resolute as our enemy
seemed to hesitate. A half hour passed away when
they again moved forward briskly to the north, and
this change of plan seemed to be the result of consultation, and led us to expect their attack through
the hollow, which it seemed their object to gain,
and by which the house was more easily assailable.
We now felt confident that some of their party

must be familiar with the ground, for no stranger would have thought of approaching through the ravine. We shifted our ground a little upon seeing this, and threw ourselves further to the right, where we still maintained the advantage of our elevated position. Learning all this manœuvring, the wives of our friends, and my mother came out, almost crazy with alarm, yet not daring to make any noise for fear of the consequences. My father peremptorily ordered them back without explanation. Our eyes were still intent on our foes, when they suddenly stopped near a spring which gushed out of the hill below us, and there remained until the moon rising higher and higher threw its clear detecting light over the scene, and discovered to us that our enemies were six of our horses that had broken loose from their pasture! What a change from the sublime to the ridiculous. In an instant we discovered the curious causes which led to our mistake. Six horses belonging to us and our neighbors had been tied together abreast, and hoppled to prevent their straying. It turned out that they had been without water for two days previously and incited by thirst, had broken into the wheatfield. In this they picked up what they could and finding their thirst increase, had followed the line of fence till they came to the one running across it.

Here they had wheeled to the right, and followed the fence until they came to the object of their search, the spring of water, where they halted, for very good reasons. While we all were truly thankful that we had no cause of fear, some of the party were almost disappointed in not being able to exchange shots, after so much excitement and such unremitting vigilance.

I have before mentioned that my father was one of those people who could be happy in the woods, and with his gun on his shoulder wander for days together in search of game,

"Fast by the forest and the limpid spring."

One morning at the time of the events I have just related, we heard distinctly as from the other side of the river the report of small arms discharged in quick succession. We rushed to the door as if in doubt whether the noise foreboded the approach of an enemy or of huntsmen. A fog hung over the water, and by intervals grew thinner or denser as the breath of morning parted it, or condensed its snowy banks. Through one of these intervals thus offered to our vision, my keen eyed mother saw a deer vigorously dashing through the water, and making for our shore. As she exclaimed aloud at what she saw, my father instantly seized his gun which hung pendant from the kitchen wall, and with the keen anticipation of sport hurried down to the river side. Sure enough he was lustily stemming the torrent, and as expressed in the words of the modern melody,

> " Wide spreading his antlers, erecting his head,
>   A stag all his enemies scorning."

As he approached, his antlers seemed larger than usual, and it was soon perceptible that he was a full grown, vigorous and powerful animal. As soon as he came near the shore my father fired, but a hesitation in his movements rendered his effort vain. The ball struck his horns, as was afterwards discovered, passed through one of them, and had broken off the prong of the other. It seemed to make no kind of impression upon him. He shook his head once, but still buffeted the waves and made steadily for the shore where my father stood, unfortunately unprepared for a second shot, and yet determined not to let the deer escape. He threw down his gun and picked up a stake that lay near him, and as the creature left the water raised his arm to give the mortal blow. What was his vexation when his weapon proved perfectly rotten and broke in pieces, without doing any injury to his antagonist, who now boldly pressed upon him, caught him between the horns, and with a desperate fury ran him against the bank. It was a criti-

cal moment, the least turn of his head would have
passed the prongs through his body. My father
here discovered his presence of mind by making
use of the very instruments of death. He seized
them fast at the ends, and converting them into
levers, their length giving him power, he succeeded
in throwing the animal on his side, and they both
fell together both panting and both remaining still
as if to gather new strength for the next encounter.
At this period of the combat, I came down from
our house attended by a hired servant, and our
astonishment was not a little excited in beholding
the situation of the combatants. We had brought
with us a fresh supply of ammunition, but it seemed
to be of little value at the critical moment. My
father cried out to his servant to take a knife out
of his pocket as he lay there and cut the stag's
throat. Unfortunately the boy had a knife of his
own, and in spite of its well known dullness, which
a sportive kitchen-maid had in pure frolic effected,
he seemed intent on making it the minister of death.
"Take my knife," cried my father. "I've got one
sir," was all the answer, and forthwith he commenced
cutting or rather scratching the throat of the pros-
trate deer. It had precisely a contrary effect from
what was intended. It produced a tickling sensation in the region of the epiglottis, which aroused

the dormant energies of the intended victim. In
an instant he was on his legs, but so was my father.
He was too keen to forego the attempt which the
stupidity of the servant rendered unavailing. A
violent effort by means of the aforesaid levers,
was again made, and the deer fearing the result,
backed off towards the water, as if determined to
make his next place of lying down not so comfortable or convenient. In spite of every effort the
deer got in deep water, and my father in letting
go his hold tumbled backwards on the shore. The
noble animal

"Up the mid stream to waft along"

made redoubled efforts, which excited our admiration, though it dashed our hopes. My father
instantly reloaded his piece and with a trembling
hand again raised it to fire. The shot took effect in
the nose of the animal, but it was not a mortal
wound. No way dismayed the gallant animal
pushed for the other shore, where he was received
with a new volley from a number of eager pursuers.
He then faced about, and attempted to swim up
the stream beyond the reach of his relentless foes.
My father followed him, and watching his opportunity came within gunshot of him, as he turned
towards a wood that came down close to the river
side. As he touched the shore he received a ball

which passed through his heart and with one lofty bound he fell lifeless on the green earth.

As my father stood exulting over his prize, he was suddenly recalled to a sense of his own injury by observing the blood trickling from his hand, and on examination discovered that it was severely wounded in this singular contest.

In 1781 troops were still continued at Saratoga, and in the private correspondence of General Schuyler and his friends, at that period it was urged as a matter of necessity. I remember a narrow escape I had, with another young person, which to this day is remembered with terror. We were in the habit of going home from the barracks in the evening, where we then were employed, and after visiting our friends, we used to take our canoe, and cross over from the eastern shore to the point near Schuyler's flats, and then walk up to the barracks. As we were always in possession of the countersign, we had no difficulty in passing the sentinels. On one occasion however during a dark night, as we approached the shore, perhaps with more carelessness than usual, in consequence of my having been with a social circle, we were hailed from the bank. Astonished at this unusual circumstance, and not being accustomed to find sentinels posted so near the water we were silent. We were again hailed

and were again silent, but in an instant the click-
ing of gun-locks announced to us our danger. I
cried, "Hold, we are friends." We were instantly
ordered to wade ashore from our boat and give ourselves up.   Unpleasant as the mandate was,
we were glad to secure our personal safety, even at
this inconvenience.   We were happily relieved
from further fears by recognizing our friends from
the barracks who were then in pursuit of some
deserters, and who fancied they heard in our conversation the voices of the absentees.   From hence-
forth we gave up our evening visits.   If I remember
right a Rhode Island regiment was then doing duty
there.

From this time to the peace, nothing occurred of
much moment to our family.   I remember the
accidental death of a party of soldiers who fell
through the ice near our house, and it was the last
incident connected with the troops which excited
our attention.   The man who drove them unfortunately directed his course towards an air hole on
the west side of the river and the whole party fell
in.   The driver got out, and with great difficulty
crept up to a hay-stack in the field by the river side,
where he passed the night without farther injury.
The other poor fellows were drowned.   When they
were taken out of the water a few days after they

presented the most horrible appearance. They appeared to have been frozen in all the different attitudes possible to be thought of, and when lying together on the ice, after they were taken out of the river, presented a spectacle which can scarce be described.

When the war was ended, I married, and with every prospect of happiness before me, removed to a beautiful farm upon the Batten kil, that to this day bears my name. Prosperity filled my sails, and when my father died, his blessings seemed to rest upon my head. But alas! time has proved how vain are our expectations. Investments which promised a certain return, melted away from my grasp. Loans which were based upon the confidence of friendship were never repaid. An unfortunate brother drew upon me for resources that I had laid up for my own declining years. In a day as it seemed, all my fair prospects vanished away. Even hope deserted me, and I have only a few more days of life to anticipate, which, while they seem a narrow space, bring with them at least the consolation of a speedy refuge from poverty and a desolate old age.

CONCLUSION.

UPON a reëxamination of the preceding reminiscences, the editor perceives many inadvertencies, and some inaccuracies, not attributable to himself, might have been avoided if he had had the leisure to examine them more attentively than it has been in his power to do.

He frankly admits that he sets forth no other claim to indulgence, than that of having preserved some minor materials to be found nowhere else, in relation to the Revolutionary War.

APPENDIX.

Lady Harriet Ackland.

GEN. Burgoyne's expedition, resulting in his capture at Saratoga, by Gen. Gates, was attended by many romantic incidents. Probably the best account of it extant is that of Mr. Street, which appeared a few years since in the *Historical Magazine*, edited and published by C. B. Richardson. But the singular fortunes of two distinguished foreign ladies of rank, whose husbands were officers under General Burgoyne, have given an interest to his career in this country which would not have been otherwise as great. The story of Lady Harriet Ackland is perhaps one of the most interesting of any connected with the personal adventures of the Revolutionary times, and has been the subject of much comment in this country and others, by biographers, poets and historians. Even the canvass was employed to perpetuate her affection for her husband, and her courage in exposing herself in her attempt to join him while he was wounded and a prisoner. The *Gentleman's Magazine* for August 1815, states that a picture of her ladyship standing in a boat, waving her pocket handkerchief as a flag of truce, was exhibited at the Royal Academy in London. Mr. Lossing in his *Pictorial Field Book of the Revolution* embellishes the 68th page of his first volume with a neat vignette of the same scene. It appears from the researches of Mr. Richardson, which were very thorough, that the received version of her career after returning home, was entirely different from the true one. That which emanated from Gen. Wilkinson, and is to be found in his curious memoirs, and which was adopted by Mr. Lossing and Mrs. Ellett, hitherto considered to be correct, is far from being so. The following appears to be the facts, and they are worthy of being annotated in this little work.

Lady Harriet was the fifth daughter of Stephen, the first Earl of Ilchester, and cousin of the celebrated Charles James Fox. Her name was Christina Caroline, and she was born in 1750, married to John Dyke Ackland, eldest son of Sir Thomas Dyke Ackland, and died in 1815 at the age of 65 years, surviving her distinguished husband 37 years. The *Gentleman's Magazine*, in its notice of her death, styled her the Right Honorable Lady Harriet Ackland, sister of the late Earl of Ilchester, and mother of Kitty who became the countess of Carnarvon. This last mentioned lady married her husband when he was only Lord Porchester, probably her cousin, and died two years before her mother. There is a curious fact worth noticing, that her eldest sister was also in the colonies, though long previous to the advent of Lady Harriet. She was the Lady Susannah Sarah, and was the wife of Wm. O'Brien who came out in 1764, and was an actor on the stage in London previously to his appearance on that of Philadelphia. In Graydon's interesting memoirs may be found a notice of this couple, to which those who are curious in biography may easily refer. She died in England, 1833. Lady Harriet's first experience of the hardships of a camp life was when she attended her husband while sick in a miserable hut at Chambly. Afterwards, when he was wounded at the battle of Hubbardton in July 1777, which was lost by our troops under Colonels Warner, Francis and Hale, and gained by Generals Frazer and Riedesel, she left Montreal where she was staying, to join him at Skenesborough. There after their reunion but a short time, their tent took fire in consequence

of the upsetting of a candle by a favorite dog. She resolved
to continue with him and share his fortunes, and was within
sound of the guns at the battle of the 7th of October when
Col. Cilley distinguished himself in a successful charge on
the British artillery, and Major Ackland was wounded and
conveyed to the rear. The enemy retiring in disorder, Lady
Harriet was obliged to take what refuge she could, among
the wounded and dying, the tents having all been struck
and scarce a shed left to shelter the unfortunate stragglers.
When she subsequently discovered that he was a prisoner
at the quarters of Gen. Poor, she resolved to go to him, and
asked permission through Lord Petersham, the aid of Gen.
Burgoyne, to repair to the American camp. This was readily
given, and a note was also addressed by him to the American
commander, asking his protection for this heroic woman.
Much as General Burgoyne afterwards indulged in literary
composition, he never surpassed the elegance of that com-
unication to Gen. Gates, written on a dirty piece of paper
and in great haste. It is still existing among the Gates papers
in the archives of the New York Historical Society. It
reads thus :

" Sir : Lady Harriet Ackland, a lady of the first distinction
of family, rank and personal virtues, is under such concern
on account of Major Ackland, her husband, wounded and a
prisoner in your hands, that I can not refuse her request to
commit her to your protection. Whatever general impropriety
there may be in persons in my situation and yours to solicit
favors, I can not see the uncommon perseverance in every
female grace and exaltation of character of this lady, and
her very hard fortune, without testifying that your attention to her will lay me under obligations.

I am, sir, your obedient servant,

J. BURGOYNE.

Armed with this note and attended by her maid, Pollard, and Mr. Brudenell the celebrated chaplain who read the funeral service of Gen. Frazer under a heavy fire of the American artillery, with her husband's valet, to attend them, drenched in a twelve hours' rain, and without food during that time, this brave lady entered a boat on the Hudson at sunset, and facing a storm of wind and waves, after a most perilous voyage reached the outposts of the Americans. Here being challenged by the sentinels, she replied in her own "clear silvery tones," the purpose of her approach, and was most kindly received by Major, afterwards General Dearborn. At his quarters she was refreshed by a cup of tea and other comforts, and informed, to her infinite satisfaction, that her husband was safe. In the morning Gen. Gates received her with parental affection and sent her to her husband's quarters, where the attached pair were once more united. After this surrender they were sent to Albany, where they received every attention from the family of Gen. Schuyler, at his mansion in the southern part of the city, which still remains in good repair, and from thence they proceeded to New York, where Major Ackland gratefully employed himself in giving relief to the American prisoners confined there, and which they much needed. Then they departed their own country, where Major Ackland was promoted to the rank of colonel and the command of a regiment. He died at his home at Pixton, in Somersetshire, on the 31st Oct., 1778, but whether from his wounds received at Saratoga or some other cause, is not clearly stated. Lady Harriet died in the year already mentioned, at her residence, Felton house, also in Somersetshire. It seems she had a son, Sir John, who succeeded to the baronetcy of his grandfather, Sir Thomas, the 7th successor, and a daughter Kitty, already mentioned, whose husband was probably her cousin and the ancestor of her present earl. Her gand-children and great-grand-childrent

LADY HARRIET ACKLAND

are now living. Apart from the great misfortune of having lost her gallant husband, she enjoyed for the latter portion of her life great tranquillity, respect and happiness. It would thus seem that the story of Colonel Ackland's duel and his loss of life in the encounter, and her becoming for a time a maniac, as well as her subsequent marriage to W. Brudenell are quite apochryphal. Romance as well as our taste is better satisfied with the truth, which is consistent with her previous devotion to her husband and the suffering she endured for him.

The Clinton and Van Schaick Manuscripts.

Governor DeWitt Clinton was not only a statesman, a naturalist and a classical scholar, but an antiquarian, and had a great regard for documents and papers relating to our ante-revolutionary and post revolutionary history. He preserved with much care the numerous papers of his father, Gen. James Clinton, and his grandfather Col. Charles Clinton, all which he had bound in several volumes and were well preserved. In these, the writer of this note found very curious letters from officials of high rank and literary personages. Among these now remembered was an autograph letter of Jane Colden the daughter of Lt. Gov. Colden, one of the most eminent savans of his day. This lady's respect for one of the favorite studies of her father, procured from his friend and correspondent Linneus the celebrated Swedish botanist, the honor of her name being given to an annual plant belonging to the 4th order. What became of these valuable manuscripts is not now known. It is to be hoped they are in good hands. Gov. Clinton's diary, continued up to the day of his death, is preserved at the N. Y. Historical

Society, and is said to have been used by the Hon. W. Campbell of Cherry Valley in his biography of the Governor.

The Van Schaick Manuscripts.

Col. Gozen Van Schaick, afterwards a general in the regular service, which rank he held at the time of his death left a quantity of papers, and letters, private and official, a large portion of which were lost or destroyed after his death by accident as is supposed. Those that were fortunately preserved consisted of letters from the Clintons, a large number of autographs from Gen. Washington of the most confidential and flattering character, showing that he held him in high estimation as a man of sound judgment as well as a gallant soldier, and others from officers under whom he served when in the provincial service, such as Sir Jeffery Amherst, which are a beautiful specimen of chirography, and to whom he owed his first commission in the British army. Among them is a characteristic letter from Gen. Montgomery containing the most humane and generous sentiments and quite a number of commissions with ponderous seals, with the autograph of George 3d, and communications from Generals Gates, Schuyler Clinton and others. What remain of this once valuable collection are carefully, reserved by his grandson Henry Van Schaick and other descendants. The copies of some of them, now for the first time in print, are subjoined.

By His Excellency Jeffery Amherst Esq; Major General,
& Commander in Chief of all His Majesty's Forces in
North America.

To Lieut: Colonel VanSchaick of the New York troops.

You are hereby Ordered & directed to march Early tomorrow morning, with Lieut: Welsh, and the Sixteen men of the above Troops mustered here this day taking under Your Care the Hospital Stores, &c. belonging to the New York Regiments, & applying to Colonel Bradstreet, who will furnish You with Waggons to transport them to Schenectady. On your Arrival at Schenectady, You will Apply to Mr. Glenn, for a Batteau, or Batteaus, if necessary, to Transport the said Stores up the River; and You will then with the Whole, & your Detachment, proceed, with the Utmost Expedition to Oswego, by the Route of Fort Stanwix, where the Commanding officer will give you Assistance in getting your stores &c. over the Carrying place.

You will receive provisions here for Your Detachment, for three days, to Compleat them to the First of July Inclusively, taking a Note from the Commissary to shew to what time You receive said provisions, by which You will be Entitled to Draw for more as they become due, at the several posts on Your Route. On Your Arrival at Oswego, You will shew these Orders to Major Duncan Commanding in Fort Ontario; and then You will with Your Detachment Join Your Regiment.

Given under my Hand at Headquarters, in Albany, this 29th Day of June 1761.

JEFF AMHERST.

By his Excellency's Command:

ARTHUR MAIR.

———

ALBANY Augst 10th

Sir

The Troops are to be forwarded to Ticonderoga as fast as they may arrive or as soon as those under your immediate command can be furnished with such articles as are absolutely necessary to enable them to take the field with this limitation — not more than 500 men in a division with an

interval of three days between each division — You will
give timely notice to Walter Livingston Esq. D : C : G : of
the Quantity of provision & number of waggons wanted for
each division — whose activity and zeal for the service will
induce him to do all in his power in forwarding this important Business, the troops to incamp at the Half Moon till
they are ready to march —— Eight days provision will be
necessary from thence to Ticonderoga. The troops will turn
off from Fort Edward to Skenesborough where boats will
be ready to receive them — the Baggage & invalid must go
by way of Fort George under a sufficient escort — A Field
officer of your regt to repair immediately to take the command at Fort George — Such sick as it may be improper to
move, must remain in this town — the Commissary, will have
care taken of them when any division marches, you will by
that conveyance inform the General, what day another division may be expected at Skenesborough that Boats may be
ordered to attend there — Shoud this be uncertain You will
advise him by way of Fort George, upon the march of a
division from hence ——

Upon Colonel Mc Dougal's arrival (who will command
during his stay here) you will make him acquainted with
these instructions & recommend it to him in my name to go
by way of Fort George lest his health so precious to the
publick shoud suffer by lying in the woods two or three
nights without a tent if he march with the men. You will
use your own discretion in determining what Companies of
your own regt, go first. I entreat you to inforce good order,
that individuals may not suffer in their property —

Let no pains be omitted to impress the men with just
notions of our duty to society — & how infamous it is in us,
who have arms in our hands for the protection of our fellow
Citizens to betray that trust, by any violation of their right —

RICHd MONTGOMERY,

LT. COLO. VAN SCHAICK.   Brigr Genl.

ALBANY 19th August 1777.

Sir

General Washington, by the Direction of the Honourable the Congress of the United States, having ordered me to take the Command of the Army in the Northern Department; I think proper to acquaint you therewith, and also with my Approbation of your Appointment to command in this City—As Colonel Cortlandts & Col. Livingston's Regiments, are hourly expected here from Peeks Kill; you will immediately upon their Arrival, inform them, that it is my orders they march as soon as convenient to the Grand Camp at, or near Half-moon; and acquaint the Commanding Officer of those two Regiments, that he apply to the Ass. D. Q. M. General, for Boats to carry the Baggage, who has my order to supply Him—The Vicinity of the Enemy to this City, renders it extremely necessary that you should observe the Exactest Discipline, and keep the most Vigilant Guard; constantly sending Patroles and Out Scouts, to prevent a sudden surprize.—You cannot be too frequent in ordering your Rounds to keep the sentrys alert; carefully attending to those who are plac'd upon the different Stores, and Magazines; You will also have a very attentive Eye to the Militia of the City, who will in every thing be directed by the Committee to Cooperate with the Continental Troops—You will continually report to me all Extraordinarys and without the least delay forward all Expresses and Intelligence to me at the Grand Camp. The Asst. D. Q. M. General, has my Orders to provide Horses and Expresses, whenever you think proper to Demand them from him—When any News or matter of Importance, is to be communicated to me, You will be careful to send it by some Officer or Express, in whom you repose the utmost Confidence. Many Misfortunes arise by employing Treacherous Persons to convey Letters —As the Militia now upon the March from the Eastern,

and Southern States arrive; You will acquaint them it is
my Orders, they do not loiter in Albany, but proceed without any unnecessary Delay to the Grand Camp   These,
with such Orders, and Directions, as you may have hereto-
fore received from the Honble. Major Gen¹ Schuyler are to
be the rule and line of your present Conduct, as Circumstances require you will receive further Directions from me—

I am Sir

Your most Obedient

Humble Servant

HORATIO GATES

Col. Goose Van Schaick, Commanding in Albany.

———

We whose Names are hereunto Subscribed, do acknowledge
to have received of Colo. Van Schaick, the sum set
against each of our Names, as part of our pay due from
the Publick.

CAMP CONTINENTAL VILAGE, 9th Octr 1778.

Benjn Hicks Capt	£48 0 0
Andrew Finch jr. Capt	48 0 0
Jno H. Wendall Capt	48 0 0
Bar. J. V. Valkenburgh Lieut	28 0 0
Adril Therwood Lieut	28 0 0
Co Sweet. Mate,	40 0 0
Jno C. Ten Broeck Lt	28 0 0
Wilhelmus Ryckman Ensign	24 0 0
Jacob F. Clark Ensign	24 0 0
Wm. Mead Surgeon	72 0 0
A. Hardenburgh Lieut	28 0 0
Jeremiah Meller Ensn	24 0 0
Christopher Miller Lieut	28 0 0

Benjamin Gilbert Ensign......................	24	0	0
Barent S. Salisbury Q. M......................	28	0	0
Nath¹ Henry L¹ while Sick at Peekskill 40			
Dollars...	16	0	0
Nicho¹ V. Rensselaer Lt......................	24	0	0
Benjⁿ Ledyard Major.........................	44	0	0
Inᵒ Graham Capt. 45 Dollars.................	10		
W. Scudder Lieut. 45 Dollars................	18		
John Ten Broeck L¹ 60 Dollars......	24		
Jacob Wendall Ensign 90 Dollʳˢ..............	36		

HEAD QRS. MIDDLE BROOK May 9th 1779

Dear Sir

I have been favored with your Letter of the 29th Ulto—

The Rifle company is to march with the troops. I did not mention it particularly, as I considered it attached to Colo Butler's Regiment and that the order for their march would comprehend it.

With respect to artillery the propriety of taking any, or how much with you, will depend and must be decided by yourself on a consideration of circumstances. If you form a junction with General Sullivan at Tioga—He will have as much with him as he shall judge necessary—Which may supersede the necessity of your carrying any; if it should be finally determined that you are to operate up the Mohawk river—it may be more material to have some with you. In either case you will consider the practicability or facility and the use of carrying it—and the smaller the number and the Lighter the pieces the better.

The Enterprize commanded by Colo Van Schaick merits my approbation and thanks—and does great honor to him and all the Officers & men engaged in it. The issue is very interesting.— I have written him a line upon the occasion.— With respect to the prisoners — I have requested General Schuyler to have such measures pursued for their effectual security — as he may deem necessary.— Their capture may prove an important event — and produce very salutary consequences — if they are securely kept.— Congress have been made acquainted with the whole of the Enterprize and its success.

I am Dr Sir

With great regard

Y^r most Obe^d Sevt

G^o WASHINGTON

BRIGAD^r GEN^l CLINTON,

(Copy.)

———

ALBANY June 15th 1782.

Sir

I lament the occasion which renders it incumbent on me to afford you a testimonial of the sense I entertain of your conduct. I sincerely wish, I could communicate it in words equal to my feelings, and to my experience of the propriety of it during a series of years.

The early decisive and active part, which you took in the favor of your country in the present Contest, justly entitles you to the attention of its Friends; we are not less indebted to your exertions as an Officer, your service whilst I had the honor of commanding the military in this Department, were such, as attracted my notice, your close attention to the discipline of your Regiment, afforded a beneficial example to officers less experienced in the duties of their offices, The alacrity with which you executed every order, The propriety of your conduct when left to act Independantly, and judge for your self, The prudence which you exhibited on occasions when the line of Conduct to be held was delicate, and important, evinsed a clearness of judgment, and a mind capable of resource, & created a confidence of which I never had occasion to Repent — Upon the whole Sir I esteem you a valuable Officer, and a faithfull servant of the Public, and should have been rejoiced, to have learnt your merit rewarded, in a promotion to that military Rank, which you claim as your due.

Delicacy would have prevented my saying thus much in a Letter to you, but to have said less, when I intend you should exhibit this to any person or persons whom you conceive may wish to be advised of the opinion I entertain of you as an Officer, and a Citizen, would have been injurious to truth.

Wishing you a speedy and an Honorable extrication from the embarassments which distress you,

I am Sir

very sincerely

your obedient

Humble servant

P. SCHUYLER.

COLO V. SCHAICK.

FINIS.

INDEX.

Canada, 44.
  expedition, 157.
Canasaraga, 151.
Capitulation, 114.
Captives, 162.
Carleton, Sir Guy, 42.
Carnarvon, Kitty, countess of, 216, 218.
Carroll, Charles, 45.
Chambly, captured, 42.
Chambly, Ackland at, 87, 216.
Chase, Samuel, 45.
Church at Saratoga saved, 90.
Cilley, Col., charges British, 217.
Clark, Ensign Jacob F., 224.
Clarke, Sir Francis, 89.
Claus, Mr., 31.
Claverack, 33.
Clinton, Col. Charles, 219.
  Col. James, 44, 45.
  De Witt, 44, 219.
  letters, 219.
  family manuscripts of, iv, 219.
  Gen. James, 142, 219.
  Gov. George, 177, 178.
  diary, 219.
Clute, Capt., finds howitzer, 139.
Cochran, Maj., 142.
Colden, Jane, letter of, 219.
  Lt. Gov., 219.
  life threatened, 11.
Congress, animosity against, 170.
Continental money, 46.
Continentals, detachment of, 25.
  accoutrements of, 26.
Cortlandt, Col., 2, 23.
Creditors to government, 103.
Crops destroyed, 86.
Crown Point, 23, 41, 177.

DEAN, Mr., interpreter, 150.
  Dearborn, Gen., 218.
  Maj. 92.
Deer, fight with, 207.
DeRuyter, Mr., 17.
DeRuyter's, 110.
Deserters captured, 79.
Desser's bay, 143.
Dieskau, Baron, 27, 29, 30.
Dovacote, 86.

Dry goods, transport of, 13.
Duncan, Maj., 221.
Dunham, Capt., 184, 195, 196, 197.

EASTERN Militia, 97.
  Ellett, Mrs., 216.
Error in pagination, 184-95.
Esopus, 124.
Evans, Lieut., 147.

FALSE alarm, 201, 202, 203-6.
  Felton house, 218.
Female heroism, 174.
Fermoy, Gen., 62.
Finch, Capt. Andrew jr., 224.
Fish creek, 148.
Fish kil, retreat to, 104.
Flag of truce fired at, 168.
Flight of families, 68, 69, 73.
Folly, Montressor's, 25.
Foraging, 99, 100.
Fort Anne, 54, 157.
Fort Brewerton, 143.
Fort Edward, 13, 64, 104, 157, 158, 222.
Fort George, 25, 26, 27, 36, 157, 222.
  hospital at, 49.
  officered by Van Schaick 137.
Fort Lawrence, 110.
Fort Ontario, 221.
Fort Plain invaded, 19.
Fort Schuyler, 142.
  Van Schaick at, 137.
Fort Stanwix, 18, 19, 125, 221.
Fort St. Frederick, 23.
Fox, Charles James, 216.
French habitans, 24.
  incursions, 17.
Frazer, Capt., 79.
Frazer, Col., 216.
Frazer, Gen., 216, 218.
  burial of, 218.
  schoolmaster, 79.

GALL, Brig. Gen., 122.
  Gates, Gen., 41, 88, 91, 99, 101, 102, 106, 114, 117, 118, 119, 215, 217, 218, 220, 224.

www.ingramcontent.com/pod-product-compliance
Lightning Source LLC
Chambersburg PA
CBHW030109030726
47498CB00007B/2317